The Half-Freaks

Nicole Cushing

New Orleans, Louisiana

The Broken Brain of Harry Meyers

"Broken"—is that the best word to use?

No.

Maybe *clammy* sums it up better. You know, sweaty. Wobbly. Sick. That's how Harry's brain feels most of the time. Like it's tilted at a thirteen-degree angle. Like it's slathered in snot. No, not snot—*mold*.

Now, granted, Harry has never actually *told me* his brain feels moldy; but I have a hunch it does. (More than just a hunch, really. Let's call it a woman's intuition.) Yes, if we sedated Harry and sawed open his skull, I believe we'd see a glob of flesh that looks exactly like long-expired lunch meat. It would be greasy, covered with tiny black splotches and thick green fuzz.

A Mystery

How, exactly, did Harry end up this way? Was his brain always moldy?

I wish I knew. Usually, my characters are pretty open about their pasts. For example, the young man in *Mr. Suicide* openly confessed that he'd wanted to kill his mother when he was ten years old. Ellie (from *The Sadist's Bible*) told me about her uptight parents, their long-standing hopes that she'd lead a conventional life, and her rote acquiescence to their wishes.

Harry, however, never talks about his childhood.

Is he hiding something from me, or is it possible he never even thinks about it? Am I expecting too much from him? Would it be normal for a man in his late fifties to confide in a woman my age, when he knows the juicy stuff might find its way into a book?

Is it possible that he has somehow gotten wind of my reputation? That he sees me as a cruel author who puts her characters through excruciating tribulations? Has he read that one review that compared me to the Marquis de Sade? Could it be that this perception makes him wary of introducing me to his younger self? Is he trying to protect that boy from my pitchfork, my pen?

Quasimodo Flintstone

I probably make it sound like Harry doesn't talk at all. But he does. Sheesh, does he ever!

It's an odd sort of talking. I don't even think of it as "talking". He's the type of person the verb "yammering" was made for. He communicates via negation (telling me what he's not, rather than what he *is*). He communicates via rhetorical questions.

Consider, for example, the following little gem he shared with me on the eve of the 2016 election: "Nah. Nah. I don't pay attention ta politics. Ya think I'm some sorta Sean Hannity?! Gettin all red faced and flustrated (sic) over that shit? Screamin my head off like some Chicken Little? Nah. Nah. I'm a workin man! After a day of rakin leaves, my back hurts too much to sit down and watch that old mummy-cunt Barbara Walters interview Nancy Reagan.

"Now, that Erin Burnett, I'd give her coochie-coo a workout. *You know* I'm the Badass Knight of Blood and Cum! Heh! But nah, I ain't the kinda fella who reads the newspaper. Not even the sports section. That's what ESPN's for. I'm just a Regular Joe, and I gotta take whatever little jobs a Regular Joe can pick up, y'know? Ya think I'm some sorta Robert Mitchum movie star?! Ya think I'm some sorta Joe Cool?! Nah. Nah. I ain't some Arthur Fonzarelli who can snap his fingers and get all the pussy in five counties. Let's get real. Uh huh. Here's a solid fact, sure as sunshine in July: I ain't gotten laid in three whole years!

"But don't ya get ta thinkin I'm a fag. Nah. Nah. I ain't. Honest!

It's just that women take a look at this face of mine and think I'm special knees (sic) or somethin. Like, maybe I got dropped on my head when I was a baby, like that Benny fella on *L.A. Law*. But I wasn't! Nah. Nah.

"I might as well be special knees, though, if folks think I look like one. Now…where was I? Talkin about Erin Burnett? Heh. Erin-Fuckin-Burnett! Yeah, I'd love to show her my king cobra—heh heh."

His tongue swings like a pendulum from profanity to euphemism, from self-deprecation to braggadocio, from past to present, from assertion to contradiction.

Sometimes Harry pops up in the corner of my office. He's not transparent, like a ghost. He's perfectly opaque and stares at me with fearful, bloodshot eyes. His eyes are his least interesting feature, though. His chin, cheekbones, and lips are far more interesting. They're what make him look like Lon Chaney's Quasimodo. Not exactly, you know. The cheekbones aren't *quite* so outrageous, the lower lip not *quite* so swollen. There's no wart covering his right eye. Nonetheless, it's the sort of face that's uncomfortable to look at.

But, at the same time, he also reminds me of Fred Flintstone. Specifically, he has a very Flintstone-esque body shape, a Flintstone-esque head of black hair, and a Flintstone-esque nose.

Quite often, he shows up to my house wearing a logo-less, dingy white T-shirt. It's frayed around the collar. Sweat has glued it onto his round belly and man boobs. Some days, however, he wears a plaid button up short-sleeved shirt that's probably close to thirty years old. Several of the buttons have fallen off, but he doesn't seem to miss them. I think he likes that shirt because it shows off his chest hair. He seems to only have one pair of pants. (Polyester.) I can't make out whether they're olive drab, navy blue, or some murky shade in between.

Sometimes, when I take a lunch break, he sits across the room from me and does the same. (He takes the liberty of making himself a peanut butter and jelly sandwich. He uses way too much jelly and it squishes out onto his paper plate.)

Other times, I feel him looking over my shoulders as I type. He leans in quite close, almost nuzzling against my neck. I think he wants to see what I'm working on. When he does that, I can smell his body odor, tooth decay, and pomade. (He doesn't wash his hair, but he uses a generous dose of hair product.)

I know he's "just" a character, but I think he pokes around in my office late at night and reads my manuscripts. Sometimes, when I walk into the office, I can smell that he's been there.

Yes, yes. He visits me.

Fabrication Nation

A problem: I've committed to writing a book about Harry Meyers, despite the fact that he's told me very little about his life. His backstory is particularly enigmatic. If we are to take seriously the maxim that "the child is the father of the man", then I am at a distinct disadvantage. How can I possibly capture the texture of his life? (Let alone its *essence*.)

A solution: What I don't know, I'll fabricate. I'll use my firsthand encounters with Harry as scaffolding to build around. My imagination will do the rest.

This is hardly an original fix for my quandary. After all, what makes fiction *fiction* is the fact that it's not *fact*. Besides, I would argue that every human being fabricates little stories about neighbors, coworkers, and even total strangers walking down the street.

A man at the grocery store wears a bushy beard, ball cap, and camouflage tank top. We say to ourselves: *He's a mechanic. A Trump voter. He doesn't read literature. I bet he doesn't even know what NPR is.* (Neglecting the possibility that he teaches college English and votes Libertarian.) A young woman wears her hair in a buzz cut and likes flannel shirts. We say to ourselves: *She's a lesbian. She voted for Hillary. She's an atheist or maybe a pagan.* (Neglecting the possibility that she's a Republican and a Catholic who shaved her head after a nasty case of lice.) An angry muscle man marches down the sidewalk, and we make up a story that he's about to get into a fist fight. (Neglecting the possibility that he's merely pissed at the grocery store for selling him rotten produce.)

We visit Canada with a certain fiction in our heads. ("They're all so polite!") Then we run into a Canadian asshole. We watch the news with a certain fiction in our heads, that the world can be neatly divided into good guys and bad guys. Then we try to ignore the fact that our hero did something villainous.

We tell ourselves that matter is solid, despite the fact that the universe is really a porous haze. We tell ourselves that no one knows what happens when we die, when in fact we know all too well. We rot. (If you have any doubt about this, bury a plastic tub of lunch meat in your backyard and dig it up again in six months. Open it, inhale its stench, and say to yourself: "*This* is what happens when we die.")

We tell ourselves that our favorite writer will be remembered forever, when in fact every writer who leaves the stage is eventually lost in the deluge of new writers looking to take their place. We dare not even consider the fact that language, as we know it, is on borrowed time. That one day, a mere two thousand years from now, no one will be able to understand Hamlet's famous soliloquy, let alone the beautiful bleakness of Ligotti. And at that point, in less than the blink of a cosmic eye, it will be as though the Bard and the Grimscribe had never been born.

This is all just a long, drawn out way of explaining that there's nothing wrong with fabricating Harry's backstory (or, for that matter, his present-day adventures). Human beings are constantly making shit up, and I am—first and foremost—a human being.

Or something darker.

Backstory (A Complete Fabrication)

Harry Meyers never married and has no prospects. In his youth he'd had a vague notion of joining the Marines, but that soon petered out. For about three months, right out of high school, he worked for a factory known as The Town Factory. His favorite part of the job was driving the forklift. It allowed him to be alone with his thoughts.

His least favorite part of the job? Anything that required him to talk to the other workers. He was poorly equipped to survive the blue-collar jungle and emerged as The Town Factory's go-to target for practical jokes and general ridicule.

For the last forty years he's worked odd jobs around the neighborhood. He'll pick up a little seasonal work on a farm, too, when things get especially tight.

He lives in the same house he's always lived in and has no plans to move. It used to be his parents' house, of course. Now that they're dead, it's his.

He resides in a town called The Town, which is located in a state called The State, which is located in a region known as The Region.

Harry's resigned to the fact that The Town is a shithole, compared to the places he sees on TV. He watches a lot of baseball games on ESPN. Sometimes, right before a commercial, they'll show footage of the city where the game is being played. (Establishing shots recorded in and around the city's landmarks or tourist sites.) He sees gap-toothed toddlers smiling and waving at the camera while St. Louis' Gateway Arch looms in the background. He sees doting dads looking on as their teenagers take paddle boats for a spin in Baltimore's Inner Harbor. He sees wholesomely-hot moms lifting up baffled infants so they can see the Liberty Bell in Philadelphia.

For Harry, Normal Places are like other worlds. Normal People are like fairies, pixies, and dwarves. These brief snippets of video before a commercial break are pretty much the only time, ever, that he's seen them. If he wasn't so stricken with painful inertness, he might decide to go to a ballgame in the nearest city. But when you grow up in The Town, you quickly learn the world is not your oyster. Yes, you can watch allegedly-important events as they sweep across the globe, but only if they're interpreted for you by someone in a distant city, speaking to you from the other side of illuminated glass.

Harry hasn't touched another human being in quite some time. His fingers might graze against those of a cashier when grabbing his receipt at The Town Supermarket, but he doesn't think that counts. Besides, now they have those automated checkout lines. When the human cashier lines overflow, six carts deep, he resorts to the automated ones because they're quicker. The trade off? Then his fingers don't even get to graze against those of the cashier.

As we'll soon see, The Town Supermarket has become a singularly distressing environment for Harry. Over the decades, he has come across many strange and terrifying sights there. During the last year, they've become more frequent and bizarre. Under such circumstances, even the smallest morsel of genuine human connection is comforting. Under such circumstances, its absence is horrific.

Our Story Begins in Earnest

One night at the hospital, about a week before Harry's mother died, a nurse approached him and spoke right into his ear. "If you want to say something to your mom, if you want to hold her, now might be a good time." Harry didn't quite realize what she was hinting at. He knew, of course, that Mother was dying. But she'd been dying for a whole year at that point, and he imagined she might go on dying for twenty more.

Mother was being cared for at a hospital called The Town Hospital. They kept her on the eastern wing of the third floor. They crammed a lot of dying people up there. "Three East," is what he heard all the nurses and orderlies and cafeteria ladies call it.

The nurse had to speak directly into Harry's ear because there were a lot of bells and chimes and blurps and beeps going off. Heart monitors, IV drips, etc. The soundtrack to slow death.

The blurps and beeps reminded Harry of the cooking timers that always blurped and beeped behind the counter at McDonald's. He ordinarily liked these kinds of sounds, because they presaged the arrival of yummy, salty refreshment. But there, in Three East, they were annoying. In the midst of all that racket, a man couldn't think.

The oxygen machine was especially annoying. It would whoosh a gust of air, and then make a brief whirring sound that reminded Harry of a roulette wheel. His mom wasn't the only patient on oxygen. He heard an inhuman chorus of at least six other, identical contraptions at work. Because they had been turned on at different times, they never whooshed and whirred *in unison*. He always heard the whoosh of air from one machine overlap with the roulette-wheel-whirring of another. Whenever he opened the door and went out into the hallway, he heard all of them at the same volume, and it seemed as if Three East were possessed by the spirit of a growling, hyperventilating animal.

Everything up there smelled like sweat, piss, shit, bleach, air freshener, musty bibles, and mildewed bones. Taken together, these scents composed the *odor* of slow death.

When the nurse talked right into Harry's ear, though, her perfume cut through all that; momentarily displaced it with the scent of flowers and candy. All of a sudden, it was like he was back in high school. Sometimes he'd get assigned to sit next to a girl, and she'd smell just like that.

"If you want to say something to your mom, if you want to hold her, now might…"

He didn't want to hold his mother. He wanted to hold the nurse.

She wasn't gorgeous, but she was young and looked like she took good care of herself. Her nails were painted the color of candy apples. Her hair was soft and shiny and black. But, much to Harry's chagrin, she looked like she wasn't that adventurous in bed. (He thought a trained eye could determine how wild a girl was in the sack, just by looking at her.)

He'd poured through a lot of porno mags over the years. Had them hid all sorts of places where Mother couldn't find them. The nurse didn't look like the kind of girl who appeared in them. Those kinds of girls were always smirking and winking at the world.

What were those smirks and winks about? Harry's theory was that the models acted that way because they knew they were desirable and the men who jerked off to them weren't. Maybe there was some truth in that, but I don't think so. I think they smirked and winked because that was what they had been coached to do. It communicated a sense of naughtiness; a sense of temptation, and surrender to temptation.

Harry decided the nurse looked more like the kind of girl you'd see interviewed on some public access TV show, while you were flipping channels between innings. The show would be about crafts or sewing or some other housewife shit, and she'd be there bragging on a project that had taken her ten years or so to finish and didn't amount to a hill of beans.

Harry decided that this, consequently, meant that her pussy wasn't shaved. In Harry's mind, only certain kinds of women shaved their pussy, and the ones who spent a lot of time sewing weren't among them. They were too busy with needles and thread to make time for razors or waxing. No, sadly, the nurse was the kind of girl who would never even *think* of undertaking such a grooming task. She probably didn't even know that some women did that. This observation made Harry feel a little sorry for her.

Harry knew, though, that *she* felt sorry for *him*. All the nurses did. He could tell by the way they talked to him. They probably thought he had "special knees", but he might be able to use that to his advantage. So what if her pussy wasn't shaved? Was that the end-all, be-all? The last girl he'd banged had a fucking Duck Dynasty beard going on down there and had just gotten out of the psych ward. And he'd had to *pay* for that. Who was he to insist on Jenna Fucking Jameson?

He thought that, if he flirted with the nurse (you know—if he gently stroked her hair or grabbed a hold of her chin), she'd probably be cool with it. She wouldn't think he was being a creep. She'd think he was being childishly awkward. He guessed she was only a b cup, but he could deal with that.

He slapped his apelike paw over her shoulder and patted it a few times. His calloused fingers rubbed her soft upper arms. He started to get a hard on. He imagined that her nipples were small and pink and that they, too, were getting harder with each passing second.

The nurse didn't yell at him, but Harry could tell she was grossed out by the whole thing. She pushed him off of her and a weird expression overtook her face; a look of simultaneous horror and relief. She looked as if she'd slammed on the brakes just in time to avoid a crash. Then she quickly shuffled out of the room.

That was the last time he touched somebody.

Obliteration

Why hadn't Harry wanted to hold his mother as she was dying? At a conscious level, he only had the vaguest sense of the answer. He suspected that if he touched her, she wouldn't feel normal. He didn't know exactly what he meant by that, but he didn't need to know. Just that thought, alone, was enough to deter him.

However, there were a few *subconscious* fears that clearly influenced the decision. For starters, the cancer had metastasized from her breast to her pancreas, resulting in a severe case of jaundice. Her face looked like a cartoon sun, and a hidden, childish part of Harry's mind worried that, if he touched her, he might burn himself. Also, she'd lost so much weight that her arthritic joints erupted from her skin, like knives. It was as if her body had begun to employ them as a self-defense mechanism. (Like a porcupine's quills, but far sharper.) A hidden, childish part of his mind worried that if he touched her, he might cut himself.

The night he stroked the nurse's upper arm was the last time he ever went to the hospital. Thereafter, instead of spending each evening visiting Mother, he spent his time in bed, watching ESPN and jacking off to *Hustler*. He liked to come on the girls' faces. His aim wasn't precise, but he usually did pretty well.

He didn't care that it messed up the picture. He ripped it out beforehand, so it wouldn't stick to the page in front of it. Then he took out a bottle of Elmer's Glue and affixed it to a piece of construction paper. That gave it some sturdiness.

Then he ejaculated on the girl's face, again and again and again for an hour or more, until it (and her neck, and maybe part of her tits) was all dried out and crusted over. In the days that followed, he targeted other areas of the model's body. Her ass. Her stomach. Her feet. Her legs. When dealing with the extremities, he would sometimes cheat a little and smear the cum around to cover any of the places he'd missed.

Only after everything else was covered did he ejaculate onto the model's shaved pussy.

He made a game of it. His goal was to saturate the girl's picture with cum, to the point where he couldn't see her anymore. Whenever he shot his load, he'd grunt "I *bury you* with my cum. I *bury you* with my cum!" In this way, Harry had begun to associate sexual pleasure with the obliteration of a woman.

Estrangement

When Mother died, Harry was the only one around to deal with the funeral arrangements. His father was in no position to help, of course. He had died many years earlier. Harry didn't know exactly when. Maybe it was when he was two years old. Maybe it was when he was three.

He couldn't remember what his father looked like, and Mother hadn't kept any pictures around. The only mental image of him that Harry could dredge up was that of a hulking silhouette that wobbled against the living room wall as Christmas lights twinkled on a tree.

Also, Harry was an only child. So, he had no siblings to share the burden. "Be grateful I had a hysterectomy right after ya was born," Mother had told him. (She said this to him way back when he was too young to understand what she meant.) "Ya get all the food and attention. I wish I'd been that lucky, when I was growin up."

Mother had one sister, a childless old maid. Even though they'd lived less than a mile from each other, they'd been estranged since before Harry was born. This aunt had been so thoroughly erased from Harry's life that he wouldn't have even known she existed if Mother hadn't taken the time, at least once a month, to denounce her as a "money-grubbing bitch".

Mother would sometimes point the aunt's house out to him as they drove back from running errands. "Look at those new shudders she had put up! Look at that satellite dish! She's livin high on the hog now, but just wait until she comes face to face with The Man Upstairs and has to explain how stingy she was to her own flesh and blood! She's gonna go to Hell for that! And that's not what *I* say, that's what *the Bible* says."

As it turned out, even if Harry's aunt hadn't been estranged, she would've been of little help with making the funeral arrangements. One of his lawn mowing customers, Mrs. Hook, once told him—out of the blue—that she used to know her. "That was before she started to go downhill. Boy, did she ever hate your mother."

Mrs. Hook went on to say that she stopped visiting when the aunt crossed the line separating senility from dementia. "I walked in one day to check on her and found her naked in the recliner. She was sittin in her own filth and tryin to shove it back up into her, well...*y'know*. I called the cops on her because I thought she needed to be put in a rubber room. But she ended up in that so-called 'Christian assisted livin program' instead. After it got closed down by The State, she was one of the ones who wandered off. Nobody ever did find her. Most folks seem to think she ran off to the woods and got attacked by an animal. Probably nothin's left now but her bones!"

Rationing Kindness

Harry was ill-equipped to handle funeral planning of any sort. If he'd had a goldfish, and that goldfish died, he probably would've found a way to fuck up the flushing. So how could he ever hope to handle a task of far greater complexity, with more significant emotional consequences?

When Mother was still alive, he subconsciously feared that her body would cut or burn him if he touched it. Those same subconscious fears haunted the day of her death, too. When his cell phone rang, and he saw it was the hospital calling, he dropped it. At the conscious level, he attributed this to being surprised and clumsy. He wasn't insightful enough to recognize that his hand had become red hot when he grabbed the phone, as if it had just been burned. That it stung, as if it had just been cut.

He let that call (and the next three from the same number) go to voicemail. He knew what those repeated calls meant. He also knew that facing such a grim announcement was beyond him. So, he crawled into the fetal position and began jerking off. His need for relief was so great that he didn't even bother to bring out his porn. He went at it with nothing but desperation to fuel his lust. It was taking much longer than usual to ejaculate. Eventually, his lower back, elbow, and wrist grew sore. He was forced to lie on his stomach and thrust his dick against the sheets. He needed an orgasm even more than he needed air.

It was at that point that he fell into a daydream.

It started with a scene set in his basement. A single dim yellow light bulb shined from the ceiling. He saw a stainless-steel coffin resting where the wood stove should've been. He opened it, found it empty, and ran his hand across the lining. The texture was breathtakingly soft and smooth. It reminded him of the nurse's upper arm.

This tactile sensation triggered a daydream-within-the-daydream: the backstory of the coffin. Harry imagined he had a guardian angel (simply named The Angel) who considered the nurse to be a stuck-up bitch for rejecting his touch. So, one night, at about three a.m., The Angel confronted her about this. Whipped out a steak knife. Flayed her milky skin off. ("If you will not allow a sad man to touch that skin, you don't deserve it!", The Angel howled.)

Then it flew away with the nurse's hide and infiltrated a coffin factory. There, The Angel magically affixed the nurse's skin to the inside of a stainless-steel job that had just come off the assembly line. Yes, her skin was indeed the coffin lining!

Harry felt his dick inch upward at the thought.

This physical sensation drew him out of the daydream-within-a-daydream (the *deeper* daydream, you could say) and catapulted him back up into the main daydream—the one in which he was standing in the basement looking at the open coffin.

He lowered his trousers and underwear down to his knees and climbed in, so he was lying on his belly. He noticed it didn't smell like formaldehyde, the way he thought it might. Nor, for that matter, was it afflicted with the odor of slow dying. It smelled, instead, like flowers and candy.

This made him rut ferociously against the lining. His tight, swollen cock slipped over the accommodating softness again and again. Each thrust drove his problems a mile away. All worry was displaced by the warm tickle of his penis head as it rubbed against the impossibly-soft flayed skin.

Unfortunately, the orgasm itself left much to be desired. (Especially given the dramatic build up.) Perhaps he should've known to expect that. Stress could affect such bodily functions. He felt a brief tingle, a throb, and a quick spurt. That was all.

The daydream was over, and he felt slightly cheated. The resulting puddle of cum was barely two inches long. Even worse, his cock stung afterward. Looking down, he could see bright red friction burns along the shrinking shaft. One of them was so severe that an odd crust had formed over it. Had that already been there when he'd started rutting against the sheets? Was it some sort of scarring? Had he been so focused on masturbation that he hadn't even noticed its side effects? He heard a faint crackling noise, and noticed this scar/sore/whatever had broken open. It seeped a thin trail of blood.

He was about to grab some toilet paper and apply pressure on the cut, but paused when the fifth call from the hospital lit up his phone. This time, he decided to answer it. (Circumstances had changed. Talking to the hospital was preferable to dealing with a chafed cock.)

It was a nurse. (Alas, not the one flayed by his guardian angel.) This nurse was a nerdy-sounding dude. He told Harry that he may want to sit down.

Mother had died four hours earlier, the dude said. No one had been able to get a hold of him, despite many attempts. As a result, the body had been taken out of the room. Did he want to come down to the morgue to "have some last moments with her" before the funeral home came to retrieve the corpse? Harry said he didn't. The whole experience was strange enough as it was. He didn't need to make it any stranger. The nurse said he needed to know which funeral home to call to pick her up. Harry said, "Whichever one's the cheapest, I suppose."

There was a long pause on the line. Harry was about to hang up, because he thought that might be the end of the conversation. *Maybe,* he thought, *they're gonna take care of everything from here on out and then send me a postcard in a few weeks sayin where she's buried.*

But then the nurse-dude broke the silence. "Just a moment please, Mr. Meyers."

Then he heard a strange variety of bleeping and blooping noises, followed by an abrupt transition to a new voice. The nerdy-sounding fellow had been replaced by a young black woman. "This is The Town Hospital's social work department," she said. "Is this Harold Meyers?"

What followed was a brief conversation about his emotional status, quickly set aside in favor of more practical matters. Did his mother have life insurance? Had Harry tucked away any money for her burial? What sort of service was he hoping for? What funeral home did his family traditionally use? Harry couldn't answer any of these questions.

And so, Mother's body remained in the morgue for two days after her death. That's how long it took for Harry to search through mountains of unopened mail, find a six-month-old account statement from an insurance company, call them to confirm that the payments since then were up to date, and reach the hospital with the news.

During the frantic search for this documentation, Harry felt tempted to just give up and hang himself. It was an idea that had occurred to him, off and on, for many years. And now more than ever he yearned for escape.

He wasn't used to diving into the heaps of mail that had grown over the coffee table, kitchen counter, and stovetop. He took for granted that they would always be there. He took for granted that they would always be more or less the same size. They had taken on a sense of permanence, not unlike the furniture and wall hangings. Tearing them apart (even out of necessity) felt like an act of wanton destruction. Maybe even sacrilege.

Another stressor was that he barely slept during those two days. Just an hour here, a few hours there. That was it.

He was always awakened by nightmares about Mother. In these nightmares, she was in a refrigerated morgue drawer, tapping out messages in Morse code; messages Harry couldn't even begin to understand.

In one particular nightmare he summoned up the courage to open her morgue drawer, but—before he could do so—a thick mist rose up from the ground and obscured his vision. His hand eventually found the drawer handle, but the mist had condensed on the metal and made it too slippery to hold on to. All the while, Mother's Morse code messages grew louder—from tapping to banging, from banging to pounding.

Perhaps worst of all, he wasn't even able to tear himself away from the mail piles for ten minutes to jerk off. This wasn't because his cock was chafed. He'd jerked off before under such circumstances and found the pain tolerable. No, it was because a queasy energy boiled over his bones. He felt feverish, chilly, and dizzy all at once. It was around this time that he started to hear Mother pounding on her metal morgue drawer even when he was awake.

He still couldn't figure out the Morse code, but it wasn't really necessary. He figured that—whatever the particulars of the message— the gist of it was that she demanded immediate release. So, he couldn't afford to take a break. He had to keep searching through the mail stacks. The sooner he got Mother out of there, the sooner she'd quiet down.

As he fidgeted over the mail pile on the kitchen counter, he stubbed his toe on the heavy toolbox he kept on the floor. As he fidgeted over the mail pile on the stovetop, he accidentally hit his head on the range hood. Also, a cold front had moved into town, worsening the arthritis in his lower back. The resulting tightness and stiffness made it feel like he was wearing a shirt two sizes too small. It had been years since he'd last heard himself scream, but the sound grew more and more familiar to him as pain collided with grief, anguish, and exhaustion.

There was a brief moment of joy (or, at least, relief) when he found the account statement from the insurance company. It turned out it wasn't in any of the piles where he thought it would be. It was in an entirely new pile that he hadn't even noticed before. (A pile that had begun to accumulate on the floor—in the space between the stove and an adjacent cabinet. Apparently, the pile of mail on the stove had grown large enough that bits of it had started slipping off into that gap.)

There was a more extended feeling of triumph when he called the 800 number on the statement. A robot voice said the policy was paid up to date and that it was worth five thousand dollars. Harry actually liked robot voices. They never screamed, nor did they make fun of him.

Of course, that was because some nerdy dude had programmed them that way. So, it wasn't exactly a virtue on their part. Harry understood that. But still, he much preferred automated menus to human beings. He possessed a surprising degree of skill in navigating them.

It was three in the morning when he confirmed the coverage, but he called the nurse's station on Three East anyway. He figured they would want to know the news as soon as he did. He could feel his pulse throbbing in his neck. His hands shook. The words stumbled and stammered out of his mouth. ("This is Har-Harry Meyers. My m-mother's in your m-morgue. I just wanted to tell ya she has life insurance.")

The girl who answered the phone sounded like she was still a teenager. She completely misunderstood what he was driving at. "We don't have anyone named Harry Meyers up on this floor," she said.

He raised his voice. "Nah. Nah. Ya didn't hear me right, woman! My *mother's* in your *morgue*. I just wanted to call and tell ya she has life insurance."

Harry heard her mutter "Psycho!" before hanging up on him.

He waited ten minutes and then called the main hospital switchboard. Asked for the morgue. Four trills on the line, and then voicemail. Some old chick (who sounded more like a cafeteria lady than a doctor) announced that he'd "reached the morgue" and that he should leave a brief message, consisting of *only* his name and phone number, after the beep.

Harry couldn't comply with this. Yes, of course, it was a simple request. But after everything that had happened, its specificity overwhelmed him. How could he limit his message to *only* a name and a number? He couldn't. He was too worked up. He needed to say more than the voicemail instructions allowed.

"This is Harry Meyers. My mother's there in the morgue. I just wanted to call and say she has life insurance." He felt tempted to keep going. Maybe ask what funeral home would work with a five-thousand-dollar policy. Maybe ask who else was being kept in the morgue alongside of her. (She once had told Harry that she never wanted to be buried next to a black person, and he imagined that such racist animosity extended to her neighbors at the morgue too.)

In the end, he decided to keep both questions bottled up deep inside of him. He'd already said too much. He should've just obeyed the instructions. From an early age he'd realized that the fewer words he spoke, the better his life seemed to go.

The social worker called Harry back in the afternoon, while he was mowing Mr. Price's lawn. He felt the buzzing in his pocket and figured he should answer. He had no desire to hear any more of Mother's Morse code messages. The sooner all of this was taken care of, the better. He stopped the mower midway through a row so he could take the call.

Even though it was only the middle of March, it was well over eighty degrees outside. And it was a swampy heat too. The sun was a mourning widow, all-but-hidden behind a veil of dark clouds. Even so, it managed to cook Harry's forehead. He panted into the phone and listened.

The social worker initially confused Harry's breathlessness with a sobbing fit. She went into tenderness mode. Used a voice that conveyed more gentleness than any other voice he'd ever heard. This lasted less than thirty seconds, though. Once she realized that he wasn't actually crying, she abruptly moved on to the task at hand. His mother would eventually need to leave the morgue and go to a funeral home. Had Harry found out more about the life insurance? Did he know who would handle the funeral?

Mr. Price (who was in failing health, himself) peeked through the curtain and stared out at his half-finished lawn. He didn't have a lot to do, so he was a bit overbearing with Harry. Any time he heard the mowing stop before he thought it should, he'd go to the window to see why. He was a frail man with rough, pale features and bright blue, scolding eyes.

The social worker raised her voice. "Harold? Harold are you there?"

Harry kept looking at Old Man Price and pointed to the phone. He even went so far as to dramatically mouth the words: "It's about Mother". That way, Price would know he was stopping for a good reason.

The social worker again: "Harold?!"

With great effort, he yanked his gaze away from Price's and directed all his attention to the phone. "Uh huh, yeah. I'm here."

"Have you found out if Dorothy had life insurance?"

"I left a message for ya about that last night."

"You did?"

"Uh huh."

"I don't think I got that."

Then he remembered he'd left the message for the morgue, not for the social worker. He explained all of that to her as best he could.

Harry heard a man's voice in the background, impatiently giving orders to the social worker. He heard the social worker mutter an unintelligible reply. Then she refocused on Harry. Her manner suddenly turned gruff, even borderline rude. "Okay. So, what's the deal? Do you have a place picked out?"

Harry let out a little chuckle that sounded like a raspy whinny.

The social worker was clearly confused by this. ("Harold? Your phone might be breaking up. I can't hear you. Harold? I need to know what's the deal about Dorothy's life insurance.")

That just made him burst forth with another chuckle-whinny. This one, longer and louder than the first.

He couldn't help it. "What's the deal?" seemed like such an odd way to phrase the question. The do-gooder instinct should've told the social worker to approach these matters with kid gloves. (Even if he wasn't crying.) After all, Harry was the lone surviving family member and obviously didn't have many coping skills. But the strain of this conversation had already tried the social worker's patience. Maybe Harry was just one of fifty bereaved family members who needed her services that day. Maybe she had to ration her empathy so it wouldn't be used up.

Harry was tempted to make a big stink about her attitude. You know, complain to her boss—the Queen of All Social Workers—and have the woman fired. But that would entail talking to even more people, and he was already feeling quite peopled-out for the day. So, he just answered her question as best he could (albeit, in a tone spiked with a shot of snark). "The *deal is* that she's dead. I'm the beneficiary of her policy. I'm gonna have about five thousand dollars coming my way, but I don't want to spend it all in one place."

The social worker said something he half-heard, but didn't comprehend. He asked her to repeat herself.

"I *said*, the least expensive funeral home in our area is Tranquility Mortuary Services."

"Trank-what?"

"*Tranquility*!!! Do you need me to spell it for you?"

"Nah. Nah. But hey, listen. Can't ya just call them yourself? Tell them to come and get her?"

The social worker heaved a sigh into the phone. "No, Mr. Meyers. I'm afraid that's not how our system works. At some hospitals, they'll call the funeral home on the family's behalf, but we've had some bad experiences with that."

That last part fascinated Harry. It stoked a fire of morbid curiosity within him. Had a scandal prompted the change? Perhaps a body lost in transit or something? His imagination began to churn away, but rather than let it run wild he decided to just come right out and ask for specifics: "*What kind* of bad experiences?"

"I don't want to get into it, sir. Now, again, the funeral home is called Tranquility Mortuary Services. It's close to the new industrial park."

The new industrial park was the latest panacea. The mayor promised it would "...cut unemployment in half and thereby lance the boil of crime that has long marred our otherwise-lovely community."

"What's their number, again?" He belatedly realized he hadn't actually asked for it before.

As she was giving him the information, he remembered he had no pen with which to record it. (Nor, for that matter, any paper to write on.) He decided not to mention that to the social worker. She was pretty frustrated with him as it was, and he didn't want to piss her off even more by making her wait ten minutes while he went into Mr. Price's house to get what he needed.

"So, you got that?"

"Uh huh," Harry lied. "I wrote it down nice and neat as can be. It's a very pretty number, too." He'd never been a convincing liar. He always said more than he needed to.

"Beg pardon, Mr. Meyers?"

"Oh, uh. Nothin."

"So, you'll call them?"

"Right after I get off the phone with ya."

Procrastination

He didn't end up calling them until later that evening. He couldn't spell "Tranquility Mortuary Services," but he remembered how it sounded. He called 411 and they gave him the number.

The man who answered the phone for the funeral home introduced himself as the owner and operator of the establishment. Harry asked him to pick up the body from the morgue, and made an appointment with him for the following afternoon. That's when they would hash out what was to be done with the remains.

Shopping

Harry decided to cancel all of the jobs he'd lined up for the next day. Even the ones in the morning, well before his appointment with the mortician. In all the commotion surrounding Mother's death, he'd forgotten to visit The Town Supermarket and stock up on essentials. He knew from experience that shopping would take hours.

He would need to sit in the parking lot for a whole hour before he even mustered up the nerve to enter the building. (He knew evil lurked within.) Then, it would take him at least ten minutes to grab a single item off the shelf, because he had to consider the pros and cons of all the different brands. (He'd be too distracted to proceed more quickly.) Then, he'd take a good half-hour to decide which checkout line to use. (He had to choose carefully, if he was to avoid a confrontation with certain entities.)

All of this relates to the "strange and terrifying sights" at the supermarket, which I mentioned earlier. So now is as good a time as any to reveal exactly what those sights *were*.

Half-Freaks!

Harry had a name for them. He thought of them as "half-freaks". They were always wandering around the aisles. They looked exactly like human beings, while at the same time looking nothing like human beings.

Some might say "half-freak" is a rude name to call someone, perhaps even a slur. But in Harry's defense he never really *called* them that. Not to their face. Nor did he share the term with anyone else. He'd never even said the word out loud. It was a label that only existed in his head. Harry knew such thoughts were better kept to oneself.

Now, you may be asking yourself: "What, exactly, did Harry mean by 'half-freaks'?"

They were misshapen in a way that went beyond mere unpleasantness. Harry himself, after all, was an *unpleasant* sight—but not in a way that made it seem like his body was at war with itself. Not in a way that made him appear to be simultaneously human and inhuman.

At least, that's what Harry thought.

To *him*, there was an exponential difference between his facial irregularities (Quasimodo Flintstone) and the uncanny valley in which the half-freaks dwelt. Personally, I agree with him. At least, somewhat. There *was* a difference between his facial unpleasantness and the radical somatic incoherence of the half-freaks. That was undeniable. But it wasn't nearly as significant a difference as he imagined it to be.

Over the years, Harry had arrived at some conclusions about The

Half-Freak Menace. For example, he discovered that each time a half-freak took a step forward (or made a movement of any kind, even a sneeze or a twitch), it caused a *half-crack* in reality.

Harry heard a certain muffled noise overhead when reality fractured. It sounded like the soft tinkle of distant breaking glass crossed with the rumble of far-away thunder. However, when he went outside after hearing the sound, he didn't see any traces of broken glass. (Or, for that matter, of a thunderstorm.) He didn't notice anything different at all! But Harry *knew*—deep in the marrow of his bones—that something was different. Oh yes!

So, you can understand why this was such a big deal. Two half-cracks would make a whole crack. And if enough of those whole-cracks formed, then who knew what would happen?! It wouldn't be good, that's for sure.

Sometimes, Harry wondered if reality had *already* shattered into pieces and if the half-freaks were just breaking it down further. He wondered (as only a *Flintstones* character would) if reality was like the rock quarry down the road. The boulders had already been broken into chunks, but the workers broke those chunks down even further, into pebbles.

Big questions to noodle through, eh? And what an unexpected place for them to be asked! The Town Supermarket was a dingy, half-derelict place where the floor was caked with grease and dust, and every can on the shelves was dented. It just goes to show that cosmic questions can erupt in the most obscure places. (Does not the word "occult" mean "hidden"?)

Because this whole deal was pretty fucking important, Harry came up with some rules for the handling of half-freak sightings.

Rules of Engagement Vis-à-Vis Half-Freaks

1.   He allowed himself only two seconds to stare at each half-freak. That was enough time to take in their ugly/awesome oddity, but not so long that they'd catch you doing it.

2.   He recorded each sighting in a notebook he kept hidden under the passenger seat of Mother's car. On each page, he wrote down the time and date of the encounter, a brief description of the anatomical irregularity, and a quick sketch of what it looked like.

So, you might be asking yourself: "What, exactly, did these half-freaks look like?"

Well, let's see... maybe the top half of their face was frozen, as still as a deer trophy, while the bottom half convulsed and slobber poured out their mouth. Or maybe the right leg of their pants was way too tight on their fat thigh, but their left pant leg sagged inward like it was almost empty.

You see, what made a half-freak a half-freak was that their body didn't quite add up. (It wasn't restricted to bodies, though. Harry reckoned that there was such a thing as a half-freak of the mind, too. But, of course, you couldn't tell if someone was a mental half-freak just by looking at them. You needed to spend some time talking with them to do that. You know, to work out which parts of their personality didn't add up.)

But anyway, let's get back to the slobbering fellow. Skeptics might say that he wasn't a half-freak at all, but that he simply had suffered nerve damage. Maybe he'd gotten a chemical burn, like the one that gave Jack Nicholson's Joker his grin. (Only, in this half-freak's case, the burn was around his eyes and nose and forehead instead of around his mouth.)

Furthermore, the empty pant leg guy—he was an amputee, right? Maybe even a war hero. Certainly not a quasi-mystical menace to reality!

This Chapter Isn't Canon

In the context of this work of fiction, Harry never even considered such rational explanations. Think about it: he had no one to whom he could confess such anxieties, and therefore no one to help rein them in.

However, I'd like to step outside the established fictional context of Harry's story, for just a moment, so I can imagine what would've happened if someone (say, for example, a psychiatrist) met Harry's concerns with skepticism.

Note: to borrow the verbiage of fan fiction writers, the following shouldn't be seen as "canon".

I see a doctor flashing a condescending grin. "Nerve damage. Amputee. That explains everything, now, doesn't it?"

I hear Harry's inappropriate response. "Nah. Nah. That don't explain shit! What do ya think I am, some sorta Mister Magoo who can't see what's in front of him? Some kinda Helen Keller with Alzheimer's? Nah. I'm a workin man who knows when shit don't add up. I saw one of 'em half-freaks a few weeks ago. The frozen-eyed, hyper-tongued type. Y'know what? That son of a bitch leaned in close and GROWLED at me! And then, (all superior-like, y'know?) he told me to move outta the way so he could grab a can of baked beans off the shelf. Well, let me tell ya Herr DOK-TOR I ain't no pussy! Nah. Nah.

What do ya think I am, some sorta sissy like Don Knotts? Nah, I didn't move outta the way. And the dude practically groped me as he reached around to grab his fuckin can of beans. A drop of the fella's drool even landed on my shoulder! Well, either that or the roof at the supermarket was leakin again. Anyhow, I got a close look at that half-freak's face. Yessiree, a *real* close look. There weren't no scars or scorched skin or none of that. Nah. Nah. No trace of a chemical burn. No trace of a good ol' fashioned fire burn, neither. Nah."

At this point, the doctor lets out a nervous little laugh and asks about "the empty pant leg" gentleman. "He's an amputee, don't you think? Perhaps even a war hero?"

Harry remains unconvinced. He explains to "Herr DOK-TOR" that he saw a half-freak of that variety a few months back. Like the slobbering man, he was going out of his way to catch Harry's eye. Harry would go to pick up a jar of Vaseline, and the dude would show up alongside him moments later, giggling. Harry would go to pick up some toilet paper, and the dude would pop up out of nowhere and let out a big old belly laugh.

"They're brazen motherfuckers," Harry hollers. "I don't even feel safe in the cash register line! Once, I thought for sure that I saw an old woman in line in front of me, gettin ready to buy tomatoes and Preparation H. But then, as soon as she finished her flirty-flirty dykey-dykey small talk with the cashier—presto!—I saw the empty pant leg guy pop up in her place. He was bendin over, wrigglin his ass like he wanted me to open up that jar of Vaseline and fuck him up the rear right there in the express lane! But it turns out that wasn't the plan.

"Nah! Nah! He was bendin over because he was diggin around in his smelly sock for some cash to pay for his Marlboros, Michelobs, and energy drinks. Now, I'm bein totally straight with ya doc, the sock he was reachin under was the sock coverin up his skinny-scrawny calf. When he reached under it, I saw a twiggy, furry, tattooed ankle. Not no artificial limb, ya unnerstand? IT WAS FLESH! Skinny-scrawny FLESH, I tell ya! And I stared at that ankle tattoo, y'know, tryin to figure out if it had any meanin. Y'know, like, what secret society it was about? I ain't never been able to solve that puzzle, though. Nah. Nah. To me, it just looked like a buncha squiggles!"

Now We're Back in Canon

Harry believed that he had seen over a hundred half-freaks over the past year. He studied them. Tried to figure out if any of them were repeat customers at The Town Supermarket. "Nah. Nah," he muttered to himself. "Each fella shows up once and only once."

He first noticed the half-freaks in The Town Supermarket way back when he worked for The Town Factory. He only saw one or two of them back in those days, and only a handful more during the decades that followed. They started to show up regularly—each and every time he walked into The Town Supermarket—when his mother was first diagnosed with The Big C. They seemed to take special delight in kicking him when he was down.

Harry worried they would eventually expand their scope of torture and start popping up in other places besides The Town Supermarket.

They did.

Life Lessons from a Half-Freak Mortician

The gentleman in charge of Tranquility Mortuary Services was skinny, old, and almost completely bald. In those respects, he was unremarkable. You might even use the phrase "straight from central casting."

Harry saw past this stereotypical appearance, though. He quickly realized it was a facade, intentionally *designed* to distract the casual observer from noticing that the old man's mouth was too small for his face. Even on a ten-year old, it would've been tiny. It was the kind of mouth that would best fit the face of a first grader.

Half-freak?

Protruding from that tiny mouth were a pair of hideous dentures. Why "hideous"? It had obviously been a long time since they'd been cleaned and, even worse, they were far too big. (In fact, they were so large that even though Harry was seated three feet away, he could clearly see hairline fractures in several of the fake teeth.)

Half-freak???

Also, the mortician's skin looked unnaturally smooth. Not at all wrinkled. But you could tell he was old: he had a shuffling gait, a creaking voice, and a remnant of gray hair along the sides of his head.

Half-freak! Oh, yes. Without a doubt. Half-freak! HALF-FREAK!

The mortician gave Harry a heavy-handed sales pitch for embalming and burial services, dismissing the more affordable option of cremation. "My dear fellow, our data shows that burial is what folks your mother's age would have wanted."

"Whuh?"

Harry knew the mortician had said something, but he'd only caught a few of the words. ("....data...burial...wanted.")

He wasn't paying attention. He was listening, instead, for the distinctive sound half-freaks made whenever they moved a muscle. (The sound of a half-*crack* being made in reality.)

The mortician repeated himself. This time, he raised his voice. He did so in the same way that many other people had raised their voice to Harry lately. Which is to say, he was clearly pissed off that he had to repeat himself, but was trying to rein in his frustration so he would still seem suitably deferential to the bereaved. Harry spied a half-snarl on his tiny lips as he bellowed, "*I said*, dear fellow, that our data shows burial is what folks your mother's age would have wanted!"

This made Harry even more suspicious. He had a theory that a half-freak might try to raise his voice so that you couldn't hear the sound of reality breaking. You could hardly blame the half-freaks for employing this tactic, but it was devilish all the same.

In any event, Harry had, indeed, heard and understood the mortician this time. But he toyed with the idea of pretending like he hadn't. Why did such a strange thought enter Harry's mind? Because he was curious to see how the mortician would react. Would he eventually start screaming? Foaming at the mouth? That might be a hoot!

Harry imagined a scenario where he would repeat, over and over again, that he couldn't hear the mortician. What would make it funny was that the mortician would have to keep up the whole dignified-and-caring routine, no matter how aggravated he got. It tickled Harry to consider just how long he could keep insisting he couldn't hear. At what point would the mortician completely lose it?

But those musings were interrupted by a noise. Not the soft tinkle of distant breaking glass and the rumble of far-away thunder, but something relatively prosaic: the sound of a frail fist rapping Morse code out on a steel table. Ah yes, the mortician had already picked up Mother! She was under the same roof as them! (No doubt in some refrigerated holding cell.) She was letting him know it was too cold in there. She wanted him to stop dawdling and start working on getting her out.

It reminded him of all the times she'd gotten locked up for DWI, and of how he'd had to run a thousand uncomfortable, bureaucratic errands (just like this one), so she could post bond.

After becoming aware of the similarity between the two situations, he decided to stop goofing off and take the conversation seriously. It was a terrible conversation to have, mostly because once a decision was made there was no going back. He thoughtfully stroked his five o'clock shadow.

The mortician adjusted his sales pitch. "I see you can appreciate what an important decision this is, dear fellow. And here at Tranquility, we understand that. We *also* understand that too few people have the difficult conversations about these sorts of things while they still can! That's why we're proud to have that data on hand that I spoke of earlier. We hired a pollster to reach out to a random sample of our town's fine residents, and find out what they want in the way of post-mortem care. That way, in cases like this where no conversation about the arrangements took place while there was still time, we can figure out the deceased's preferences based on their demographics!"

The phrase "post-mortem care" struck Harry as an unnatural one. He'd never heard it before, and wanted to ask the mortician exactly what that entailed. But then Mother's rapping grew more frequent and hostile. It was even, for the first time, joined by the marrow-piercing sound of her nails scratching against the steel table. Surely, the mortician heard her!

But he did a good job of pretending he hadn't, and Harry knew he would come across as batshit loony toons if he addressed it. So, he kept listening.

"Now, would you be surprised, dear fellow, to learn that a clear majority of folks in our town—regardless of age—prefer a traditional Christian burial to cremation?" He pulled out a blurry, mimeographed pie chart that Harry couldn't quite understand. There was no text on it, as far as Harry could tell. Also, if he was reading it correctly, there wasn't any one, significant chunk of the pie that was overwhelmingly larger than the others. To the contrary, all the pieces were nothing more than tiny slivers.

A thought suddenly occurred to Harry. *Tiny slivers of pie, all the better to fit into a tiny mouth!* I'm sure that you and I, reader and writer, will agree that this was a nonsensical thought. For Harry, though, it was a thought that made quite a bit of sense. The misshapen nature of half-freaks carried over into their work. Their slightest movements made half-cracks in reality. Therefore, it should be expected that any fruit of their labor would be slightly unreal. If a half-freak was a butcher, he'd produce slightly unreal beef. If a half-freak was a baker, he'd produce slightly unreal bread. If a half-freak created a chart to sell embalming services, he'd produce a slightly unreal chart.

However, Harry couldn't let the mortician know he'd arrived at that conclusion. It would be giving too much away. So, he played dumb, and shrugged, and said, "Nah. Nah. I suppose I wouldn't be too surprised by that."

The mortician grinned. Strings of spit gave his dingy dentures some luster. "Smart boy. Now, the chart I just showed you was generated by our analysis of the responses of a random sample of *all* town residents. From age ten all the way up to age one hundred and ten! But if we zero in on your mother's specific demographic cohort, your best course of action becomes even clearer!" He pulled out another blurry, mimeographed pie chart. This one, at least, was clearly labeled. ("Post-Mortem Care Preferences of Caucasian High School Dropouts, Age 70-75.") But the pie itself, so to speak, was marred by a half dozen stains. (Smudged ink, drool, coffee, blood, etc.) They made it difficult to confirm that the chart said what the mortician claimed.

The mortician beamed. "An astounding *one hundred percent* of respondents in your mother's cohort preferred Christian burial to cremation! So, even though you weren't able to broach that delicate subject while she was still living, I've been able to essentially *broach it for you* using the latest state of the art polling techniques. Using the science of public opinion research, we can assure you of what she would have told you to do, if you'd asked her. We give the dead their voices back!"

Harry Resists the Sales Pitch and Opts for Cremation

The reasons for his decision were as follows.

1. The mortician was a half-freak. Half-freaks were not to be trusted. (I mean, *come on*, their apparent mission was to break reality apart!) If you were in Harry's shoes, would you cave in to the mortician's high-pressure pitch? I don't think so!

2. When he mulled over the possible motives behind the half-freaks' plan, it occurred to Harry that they might be aliens. The ongoing, gradual destruction of reality could be the first sign of invasion! At first this may sound absurd (it did to me). But the more I think about it, the more it makes sense. Perhaps the aliens came from a planet where intelligent life isn't structured symmetrically, as it is on Earth. Perhaps they came from another dimension where symmetry doesn't even *exist*. So, when they created their humanoid disguises, the bodies didn't quite add up. If this were true, then Harry's resistance to the mortician's sales pitch would be far more than an exercise in frugality. It'd be a sign of heroism! By daring to say no, Harry demonstrated that human beings (or, at the very least, "workin men") weren't pushovers. He was making a statement about the toughness of the human race.

3. You will recall that, in the hospital, his mother's face looked like a cartoon sun, and a hidden, childish part of his mind worried

that, if he touched her, he might burn himself. This image—nestled deep inside Harry's subconscious—destined Mother to cremation. *Mother = fire.*

A Nap

Harry felt drained after his appointment with the mortician. This, of course, was an entirely normal way to feel after such a conversation. Talking about money is draining. Ditto for talking about death. The intersection of the two? Well, that would be a place of piercing fatigue, wouldn't it? Even under the best of circumstances.

And, of course, these were far from the best of circumstances. He'd had to insist on cremation, over and over. He'd had to shove aside poorly mimeographed pie charts and reject the mystical powers of data. He'd had to tell the mortician, in no uncertain terms, that he didn't want to spend $5,001—the quoted price—when he could give Mother to the flames for a fraction of the cost. ("What do ya think I am, mister, some kinda Bill Gates with billion-dollar bills gushin outta my eyeballs? Some sorta Levon [sic] Musk with a car travelin in space?! Nah. Nah. I'm a workin man, and I can't spend all that money on fancy-ass embalmin and a fancy-ass coffin. Nah. Nah. I can't go for that. No can do!")

The mortician had pretended not to hear him, and tried to rush him out the door with an "enforceable verbal agreement for full Christian burial". That's when Harry raised his voice and made a fist. "I know your secret. I know what you're up to!" he'd shouted. "Ya won't win, ya hear me? Ya won't WIN!"

The mortician then threw his hands up and began to quake, dramatically, in a way that could be interpreted as a parody of fear. "Okay," the half-freak whispered. He appeared to be on the brink of a giggling fit. "I relent. Go ahead and just toss aside the blessings of data-driven decision making! Make your own decision. I guarantee that you'll regret it."

In short, it had been an ugly scene between two ugly men, over an ugly matter, being contested in an ugly town. I think you'll agree that this aggregation of ugliness created a situation that was uniquely draining. Indeed, it would have driven any number of men mad!

So it was that when Harry returned home, he waddled up the creaky stairs, collapsed on his bed, and hid under a pile of long-unwashed, sour-smelling sheets. Within moments, he was asleep.

Harry's Prophetic Dream

It started with Harry in the kitchen, making himself a peanut butter and jelly sandwich. A funny smell drifted up from the basement. No, not the smell of decay. (Although that was a very good guess.) It was, rather, the smell of burning plastic. In fact, Harry initially thought someone was in his basement smoking crack, because he knew a neighbor who got hooked on that shit thirty years ago. A guy named Andy. He'd smelled it when he mowed the dude's lawn.

Andy eventually moved away from The Town (as many people do). Years later, though, Mrs. Hook told Harry that the poor guy ended up hanging himself in prison.

So, in the dream, Harry tramped down to the basement to see if maybe Andy had come back from the dead (as many people do, in dreams). He wanted to ask the corpse what he'd done to get locked up, and if prison had really been all that bad. He wanted to ask the corpse if there was any pain involved in hanging oneself.

Alas, those questions would have to go unanswered. It turned out Andy was not there.

A single dim yellow light bulb shined from the ceiling, but the basement was also illuminated by flames. A gray plastic coffin (made to look as if it were stainless steel) rested where the wood stove should've been, and it was burning. In the midst of the half-real flames and half-fake smoke, a choir of tall, white-robed angels sang a jubilant anthem; a song of triumph and determination, swiped with impunity from the catalogue of a classic rock band. They squeezed huge bellows as they sang, to help the fire grow. Tiny cherubs flitted about, as well, tossing confetti-like diamonds into the air, each of which caught the firelight and sparkled.

Then Harry heard a voice which he understood to be the voice of Christ. "Blessed are the cremators," He said, "for they...for they...for they....".

Christ, it turned out, wasn't Christ at all, but a recorded voice on a skipping record album.

"....for they....for they....for they...for they..."

For some reason Harry couldn't quite put his finger on, this turn of events seemed infinitely terrible. His intuition turned out to be correct.

The burning coffin lid suddenly snapped open, apparently in response to a howling wind that wanted out. It whipped around the basement like a tornado, flinging dust and mouse shit and slivers of stone through the air. And in that howling he heard Mother's voice (phlegm-congested, fragile, and only half-familiar) wailing: "She's with me and she's scared! She's with me and she's scared!"

Then came the storm clouds, and a monsoon broke out in the basement. (Even as the little rectangular windows near the ceiling revealed sunshine outside.) The Angels, cherubs, and diamonds all began to dissolve like so much sugar. The casket-fire sputtered and drowned. As for the casket itself, a trap door opened underneath it, sending Mother and her mysterious, frightened fellow traveler plummeting down into a pit of writhing worms.

The Half-Freak Mortician Claims the Remains *Must* Be Buried Because
His Cremation Oven Broke Down

As you can imagine, this was not the news Harry wanted to hear. Honestly, Harry really didn't care to hear any more news *at all* about his mother's remains. He would've preferred for the cremation to have gone off without a hitch and for the ashes to be used as fertilizer to keep the lawn of Tranquility Mortuary Services a healthy, lustrous green. He would've liked for the thousand-dollar fee to come out of his bank account as a one-time, automatic debit, so he'd never even have to see a bill.

He would've preferred for things to go that way, because then it might have been possible for him to imagine that he'd never had a mother at all. (And under such circumstances, her absence wouldn't hurt so much, you see.) Hell, if he'd really put some effort into it, he might've been able to convince himself that *no one* had ever had a mother; that such creatures were the stuff of myth, that they weren't the source of life, that there were no such things as babies, that everyone and everything just sort of faded in and out of existence for no apparent reason.

Harry found out about the alleged malfunction by way of a phone call in the middle of the night. (3:47 a.m., if you must know the exact time.)

The old mortician himself was the one who made the call. "Dear fellow, I'm terribly sorry to awaken you at this early-late hour, but I feel an obligation to inform you that an unavoidable mechanical issue has resulted in your mother only being...well...*half*-cremated. That is, her right-hand side has been turned to dust but her left-hand side remains

61

intact. So, you see, we'll have to *embalm* the half that remains intact and bury it along with the ashes of the other half. May I suggest Tranquility Cemetery as the post-mortem housing provider for your mother? May I consider this call a binding verbal contract for the order of a burial vault from Tranquility Crushed Stone and Concrete?"

Harry wished he hadn't picked up the phone. He wished he'd never chosen Tranquility Mortuary Service to handle his mother's "post-mortem care" needs. He wished he'd never talked to that one particular social worker (the one who'd referred him to Tranquility), and that his mother had never ended up in that particular hospital, and that she hadn't gotten that particular variety of cancer, with that particular series of metastases. He wished she'd never gotten cancer at all. He wished she'd died when he was too young to really remember her, the same way his father had.

These wishes, of course, could never be realized. They fell, defeated, one by one, like dominoes. Only, they weren't a *straight line* of dominoes that eventually came to a stop.

No, they were arranged in a circle, and made of rubber. (Or, at least, made of *some sort of material* that possessed a property of exuberant bounciness.) The point is, these mental dominoes sprang back up into position mere moments after they'd been knocked down. The wishes wouldn't stay dead. They were constantly rising up and falling down, over and over and over and over and over.

This is what Hell must look like: a series of increasingly desperate wishes, knocked down and risen up again, ad infinitum. A perpetual yearning machine.

What does that say about me, that I put Harry in such a hellish situation? Am I the Devil? Or, at least, *Harry's* Devil? My name is Nicole, after all, and "Old Nick" is an alternate name for the Devil. But if I were the Devil, wouldn't I already know it?

I don't know the answers to such questions. I don't *want* to know the answers to such questions. So, I'm going to change the subject.

You're probably wondering what Harry said to the mortician.

Well, for a long, long time (possibly five minutes, maybe even ten), he didn't say a word. He remained silent, and the mortician remained silent. It was a stand-off of silence. He and the mortician were like two opposing western gunfighters. Or, perhaps it's better to compare them to opponents in a chess match. I don't believe Harry ever played chess, so the comparison probably never occurred to him. But when I look at this situation, that's the sort of tense atmosphere I imagine. Neither one of them said a word, because they knew Harry's next move would carry momentous consequences.

Finally, Harry spoke. "Nah. Nah. I ain't givin ya my verbal permission to do sh—." He was on the verge of cussing, but stepped away from that particular ledge.

A new realization occurred to him, quite out of nowhere: to win the competition, he would need to speak in a more dignified manner. If he cussed, he would be projecting weakness (the mortician seemed to derive satisfaction from getting him all riled up). To deprive him of that satisfaction, Harry addressed him politely, the way one businessman addressed another on old TV shows like *L.A. Law*.

"Nah, I mean, um...No.," Harry said (trying his best to sound well...*tranquil*). "You don't have that permission. I'm a working man, with a set of tools that I can bring over. What do you say I come by bright and early at nine o'clock and see if I can fix that cremation oven for you?"

The mortician didn't respond. He let out a sound that might have been a groan, then he hung up. Apparently, Harry's chutzpah left him speechless. He was forced to retreat.

I don't blame the mortician. I can totally relate. I'm a bit stunned, myself, that Harry went on the offensive like that. I can only explain this turn of events by reminding you that everyone has their breaking point. This was a *Popeye*-like moment in which Harry said to himself something along the lines of, "That's all I can stands, I can't stands no more."

Bear in mind, Harry had been ridiculed and excluded all his life. Now he found himself faced with the death of the woman who, for better or worse, anchored him to the world. Without her, he was adrift. And how did The Town respond?

By flinching away in disgust when he tried to touch them.

By only offering him a business-like, bare minimum ration of kindness.

By trying to push unnecessary funeral expenses on him.

By mocking his refusal of the sales pitch, and making up a crazy story (a broken-down cremation oven!) so they could still get their way.

By allowing the half-freak menace to incubate freely, without opposition.

And so, Harry fought back. He finally realized, if only subconsciously, that there were two ways to experience the world. The first way, the one he'd known for most of his life, was to resign himself to a total lack of autonomy. The second way, the way he was trying out now for the first time ever, was to seize autonomy by any means necessary. (Even if that meant fabricating it out of whole cloth.)

By asserting, without a shred of evidence, that he could perform a repair that he was in no way trained to perform, he would be calling the mortician's bluff. (Meaning that the mortician would be compelled, by the necessity of etiquette, to show Harry the cremation oven.)

Given that access, Harry would be able to expose the mortician's fraud. He would demonstrate that the oven was, in fact, working without a hitch and had never been in need of repair. Of course, for this ploy to work, Harry would need to know how to turn on a cremation oven.

Jitters

This should've been the hour of Harry's triumph. He should've felt empowered to strut around the house with a shit-eating grin on his face and have a peanut butter and jelly sandwich to celebrate his victory. But instead, confidence suddenly fled from him, like a tide retreating back to sea.

Why did Harry's confidence suddenly flee from him? I think there were a couple of factors.

While it was true that he had taken a considerable step forward by defeating the mortician at his own game (that is, The Game of Making Intentionally Awkward, Outrageous Claims), he had only done so *over the phone.* He knew that it would be much more difficult to prevail in direct, face to face combat at the funeral home (where the mortician held home field advantage).

Also, he wasn't sure he could figure out how to turn on a cremation oven. He had no idea what the control panel even looked like. Would it be as simple as finding an "on" switch and flipping it? Or, given the gravity of such a task, would two authorizations be needed? (Like when they decided to self-destruct the *U.S.S. Enterprise* in *Star Trek*?) Would a key somehow be involved? A digital code?

Those were the worries that made Harry's heart sick. In fact, if we had been there with him at that early-late hour, armed with a scalpel to slice open his furry chest, and if we had cracked open his sternum with a giant crab mallet, so that we could gaze directly at his heart, we would've seen that it looked clammy. You know, sweaty. Wobbly. We would've noticed that it was tilted at a thirteen-degree angle and slathered in snot. (No, not snot—*mold*.)

If Harry had been like other twenty-first century Americans, all he would've had to do is yell out "Hey Alexa (or Siri), how do cremation ovens work?". But he didn't have Alexa or Siri. Hell, he didn't even have a computer, tablet, or smartphone. Mother didn't care for such innovations. "If ya think The Town Factory was bad," she had once said, "the last thing ya need to do is get all wrapped up in this cyber-bullyin I hear so much about. Nah. Nah. My son don't need to get tortured like that!" She'd wrinkled up her nose in a very peculiar way during that lecture, the way she always did when she was over-excited. Also, her neck had seemed to swell out, like that of a ribbiting frog.

In fact, she'd only grudgingly given her permission for Harry to get a flip phone. (He was able to make the case that it was a business necessity. A "workin man" needed a way for customers to reach him.)

He paced across the bedroom. His stubby fingers played with his stiff hair. He remembered that Mother had kept an early '70s set of the *Encyclopedia Britannica* boxed up in the basement. Surely an encyclopedia would have something to say about the workings of a cremation oven, wouldn't it?

Alas, Harry would never find out. He was too nervous to go down there. (What if a plastic coffin was down there, where the wood stove was supposed to be? What if Mother was in there, waiting to suddenly pop up and scare him like the rotten little cackling dude in *Tales from the Crypt*?)

He was a grown man. Yes, yes. *More* than just a grown man! At some restaurants he qualified for the senior citizen discount! Yet there he was, frightened of his mother and of the basement and of The Cryptkeeper. *What kinda wimp am I turning into?* The question hit his moldy brain hard, smooshing it in like a pumpkin long-gone-bad.

Rage was the only cure for self-loathing that Harry had ever known. And so, he found himself at another, very different, breaking point. He was no longer Popeye, energized to kick ass. He was a toddler running amok through every room in the house, throwing a tantrum. It went on for well over an hour.

He kicked over huge stacks of unopened mail, and felt disappointed because they gave way so easily and made little noise when they fell. So, he moved on to kicking over plastic trash cans, and found toppling them to be a bit more satisfying. They made *cah-lunk*-ing sounds when they fell. He imagined each *cah-lunk* was a groan of pain.

He punched holes in the drywall, but hurt his fist in the process. He wanted to cry, and that made him feel ashamed. He bit the injured fist. He hoped that it would respond to the punishment by toughening up.

Then, for quite a while, he walked around in a daze. At first, he was aware of a gentle wobbling sensation, but soon all awareness faded away. When he came to, his back stung like a motherfucker. He'd been flagellating himself with a leather belt.

Even though no one else was in the house, he felt embarrassed. He flung down the belt like a hot potato, tore a leg off the coffee table, and threw it at one of the holes in the wall. He wanted to see it get bigger, but didn't want to punch it again. That plan backfired. The leg of the coffee table bounced off the wall and hit him in the chin. He responded by flinging a work boot at the kitchen window. He wanted to see it crack. It didn't.

By this time, you see, Harry was growing tired. While he was indeed "a workin man", his labor required him only to make a handful of repetitive movements. What I'm driving at is simply this: one needn't be particularly athletic to push a lawnmower around all day. Harry was living proof of this.

Tearing apart a house, though? A fellow needed flexible tendons and fine-tuned muscles if he was going to perform that task to completion.

Harry just wasn't up to it.

He collapsed onto the floor and burst into tears. He couldn't hold them in anymore. He felt a warm stickiness invade his trousers. (Yes, he was still wearing trousers. He never bothered to change out of his clothes to go to bed. But that's a story for another time. The main point is, this self-described "Badass Knight of Blood and Cum" had pissed his pants.)

He tried to let out a full-throated scream, but found himself failing at even that simple act. He had too much slobber in his mouth at the time, so he ended up forming a spit bubble and making a low, gurgling growl.

Still wearing his urine-soaked slacks and underwear, he waddled back upstairs to his bedroom. There, he unbuttoned his fly, unzipped his zipper, and pulled his trousers and underwear down around his ankles in one fell swoop. Of course, you realize he wasn't doing this so he could begin cleaning himself up. He was doing it so he could masturbate. It was the only coping mechanism he had left.

He tried to shake the humid, unbearable sense of failure off his shoulders. He tried to conjure up a mental image of the nurse with the soft upper arm. The image appeared, crisp and clean. In this mental-movie, she was naked, bruised, and humiliated. She was begging to be given the honor of sucking Harry off. But even then, while resting in bed under the influence of an exquisite daydream, Harry's cock refused to stiffen.

Outside, in the predawn dark, children waiting for a school bus let loose a volley of malicious belly laughs and snorting giggles. Immediately thereafter, he heard reality cracking. (That is, a series of *half*-cracks ensued, occurring more or less simultaneously, thus creating numerous *full* cracks.)

As you may recall from earlier in the story, half-cracks sound like the soft tinkle of breaking glass crossed with the rumble of far-away thunder. For the sake of brevity, I propose that we shorten this description to: *softtinkle, rumblethunder.*

That was the noise Harry heard outside his window, over and over in rapid succession, when the children laughed.

Softtinkle, rumblethunder.

Softtinkle, rumblethunder.

Softtinkle, rumblethunder.

Softtinkle, rumblethunder.

Softtinkle, rumblethun…

I'm not one hundred percent sure if Harry was strong enough, at that point, to roar out loud, but I do know that—at the very least—he roared in his head. He roared and thought to himself: *The kids are half-freaks too? How long can this go on, before everything falls apart?*

He wished he had binoculars. Perhaps then he could've crawled to the window, parted the mini blinds, and taken a long hard look at their faces (to detect, for example, if their mouths were too small, or if their legs were of unequal thickness).

Hmmm. Let me pause to think for a moment. Did he *really* wish he had binoculars so he could determine if the kids were half-freaks? Or, was he merely using his lack of binoculars as a convenient excuse to *not* look? (Yes, of course, he was upstairs and they were on the street, but the house only had two stories. It's not like he was living in a penthouse and actually *needed* binoculars to observe kids in the street!)

I think he *half*-wished he had binoculars.

Altered States

Harry remembers the '80s film *Altered States*, starring William Hurt as a scientist whose experiments with a sensory deprivation tank and hallucinogenic drugs make him physically devolve into a prehistoric ape-man.

Well, to be honest, Harry doesn't remember the film in its entirety. You see, he's never *seen it* in its entirety. For that matter, he didn't even see it *in the theater*. (Mother didn't approve of theaters.) Nor did he catch it on VHS. (Mother thought renting movies was a waste of money when there were so many programs available for free on television.)

He saw it on a UHF channel, back around '84 or '85. They were playing it on a rainy Saturday afternoon. The movie had already started when he tuned in. Mother was passed out after a binge, so there was no risk of her making him change the channel. The drug use itself would've been enough to make her flip out. She shielded Harry from any form of entertainment that might, in her opinion, glamorize such behavior.

She didn't see the hypocrisy in ranting against drugs on television while ignoring her own very real substance abuse issue. She had been hypocritical, in that way, for so long that it seemed completely natural to her. Some people are born with hypocrisy sewn into their soul. They can't escape from it. It defines them. Harry's mother was such a woman.

The only parts Harry remembered were the isolation tank and transformation sequences; the scenes which gave him feverish daydreams and corpse-cold nightmares for weeks afterward.

You may be wondering why I've chosen to mention all of this, at this particular point in the story. You may be thinking to yourself: *I don't give a damn that Harry saw* Altered States *on TV when he was a young man. I just want to know if he foiled the treachery of the half-freak mortician!*

Yes, you were thinking something like that, weren't you?

Well, you see, the reason I'm mentioning *Altered States* is that images from the movie popped into Harry's head that morning. He knew the bus stop children had been laughing at *him*. (*They must've been able to see through walls or somethin*, Harry thought.) This realization triggered something akin to a panic attack, and the panic attack triggered thoughts of how great it would be to spend time in an isolation tank, like the one in the movie. If he changed into an ape-man, like William Hurt had, then none of this would bother him. He would be able to intimidate anyone who crossed his path.

After all, nobody had laughed at William Hurt, had they? Nobody had tried to upsell him into buying a "full Christian burial" package for his mother, had they?

Not in *Altered States*, they hadn't. At least, not in any of the scenes Harry remembered.

It was this train of thought that led him to finally step out of his piss-soaked underwear and trousers (which had remained down around his ankles during this rumination), remove his shirt, and stagger downstairs to the bathtub. It wasn't an isolation tank, but it would have to do.

Harry's bathroom smelled like an equal mixture of soap and mildew, but the water soothed him. He tried to imagine it was an isolation tank. Alas, his brain couldn't manage that for some reason. Instead, he ended up imagining he was in his mother's womb.

It's a cliché, of course, to say that someone was "sleeping like a baby". But Harry did fall asleep in the bathtub, and it was a deep, dreamless sleep.

Don't worry—he didn't drown in there. His head remained comfortably perched on the tile wall. He simply slept, and his sleep was even better than that of a baby. He was sleeping *like a fetus*.

The Sky Is Falling

Like most residents of The Town, Harry heard the sky falling before he saw it. The noise could best be described as that of a grinding, sputtering galactic engine (to paraphrase Allen Ginsberg, an oil-less dynamo in the machinery of morning) combined with the sound of a thousand baboon shrieks played backwards. For the sake of brevity, this combination of sounds will be presented from here on out as: *starsputter-grind, 1,000 noobab skeirhs.*

If there were any normal people left in The Town, and if they were Christian fundamentalists, they might have thought the sound was that of an angel trumpeting the arrival of Judgement Day. (It didn't sound anything like a trumpet, really, but a religious mind could have talked itself into believing it was a trumpet. After all, wouldn't a heavenly trumpet sound different from an earthly one?)

But let's bring this back to Harry Meyers. This might surprise you, but he wasn't a Christian fundamentalist.

Of course, he'd gone through the motions of prayer and praise when he'd visited Mother's holy roller church on Christmas and Easter, but he didn't actually *believe* all that stuff. At the same time, though, he wouldn't have called himself an atheist. (I can just imagine his objections to *that* label: "Nah. Nah. I ain't no atheist! What do ya think I am, some sorta Madeline Murphy O'Harrah [sic]? Some sorta pencil necked geek college perfessor? Nah! I'm a workin man…")

Instead, the whole thing seemed irrelevant to him. His world was mowing lawns and going to the grocery store and watching ESPN and eating peanut butter and jelly sandwiches and masturbating. Religion didn't have a whole lot to do with any of those interests.

Now, yes, he *did* believe in half-freaks. But they could hardly be thought of as deities. I suppose if he believed in anything else out of the ordinary, it was aliens. When he wasn't watching ESPN, he liked watching UFO shows on The History Channel. And—if you'll recall—it did occur to him earlier that the half-freaks might be an advance party of aliens looking to invade Earth.

So, when he abruptly woke up in the bathtub (some four hours after having fallen asleep, with wrinkly fingers and toes to prove it), he thought the horrible sound might be a landing alien armada.

He stood up and slid open the frosted bathroom window. He saw no spaceships, just a square fragment of blue sky accelerating toward the ground, and a gaping black void indicating the place it had once occupied. The sky-against-sky friction generated sparks, but the fragment didn't burn.

Harry couldn't see exactly where it was heading, but when it landed (with a bomb-like boom) the earth shook, and the bathroom tiles all bucked like so many broncos. This unsteadiness worsened with each passing second. The floor writhed and churned. It was as if Harry were on a boat, sloshing right and left, up and down, all at once.

He heard pipes breaking inside the bathroom walls. He heard a clatter upstairs, and suspected a section of ceiling had given way (as if to imitate its big sister, the sky). Lights flickered and kept flickering. They were indecisive lights, vacillating between staying on the job and calling it a day.

The mayhem would require him to once again cancel all his lawn mowing jobs. (For the second day in a row!) He reached for his flip phone.

Then (and only then) did he remember last night's phone call with the half-freak mortician. He looked at the phone and screamed. He'd said he'd be at Tranquility Mortuary Services to fix their cremation oven at nine a.m.

The time was ten-thirty.

Twenty Percent Sincere

Harry tried to reach the mortician via phone, but the call went straight to voicemail. "You're probably wonderin where I'm at," Harry yelled. (Another piece of sky had started to fall, with all the corresponding racket.) "It ain't that I'm chicken, ya unnerstand that? Nah. Nah. I ain't scared of any technical issue with cremation ovens. I'll have it fixed in a jiffy. I've fixed a thousand of em before. That used to be my job, y'know, fixin cremat—".

The voicemail beeped and a robot voice gave Harry an abrupt dismissal. "Thank you for calling. Goodbye." Then, a loud dial tone.

Harry knew that only one of those five words had been sincere. Even the robot voices had rejected him. He threw the phone down onto the wiggling tile. It shattered into a thousand glass and plastic and wire pieces. Some of those pieces bounced back off the floor and hit his thigh and belly, but it was worth it.

Why Harry Didn't Hang Himself

At this juncture, you may be asking yourself why Harry didn't just hang himself.

After all, the sky was *literally* falling. Robot voices had betrayed him. He'd suddenly lost the ability to get an erection. Worst of all (yes, even for Harry there were worse things than not being able to pop a boner), any chance he'd had to outsmart the half-freak mortician passed him by when he didn't show up at Tranquility Mortuary Services at nine a.m.

Harry imagined the mortician looking on cheerfully as the clock advanced from 9:00 to 9:01, to 9:05, to 9:20, etc. In his mind's eye, he saw his nemesis rubbing his too-smooth hands together and gleefully picking up a shovel. He suspected that the old charlatan wasn't even going to embalm Mother. He'd just toss her in some pit and send Harry a fraudulent bill.

Harry imagined what it would be like to confront the mortician in the wake of such chicanery. The scoundrel's rationalization would go something like this: "What else was I supposed to do, when you failed to show up to fix the oven? (Guilt trip.) I couldn't very well let her linger in my freezer for days. That would be an uncaring way for me to act, don't you think? To let her linger unburied for days, I mean. Especially since I understand she had to wait several days before leaving the hospital morgue. (Another Guilt Trip.) Moreover, did you know that Town citizens of her demographic, without exception, told our pollsters that they prefer a proper Christian burial to cremation? ('Data' that was probably fabricated out of whole cloth.) I did show you the charts about that research, didn't I? (Bleeding ink charts. Stained charts. Illegible charts.) Am I not correct in remembering that we had a binding verbal contract to go ahead with full Christian burial? (An outright lie.) Isn't all this cremation mumbo-jumbo a last minute change, quite out of the blue, and therefore in violation of our binding verbal contract?" (A particularly brazen lie.)

What could he do to overcome such shrewdness?

Nothing, absolutely nothing. He would have been powerless over it, even before the sky had started falling.

But sometimes, futile resistance is its own reward. Maybe, Harry thought, it didn't matter so much whether he was ultimately able to stop the mortician from defrauding him. The mere act of resisting might give him a place of honor in future history books as a sort of anti-half-freak guerilla. And he'd rather be known as a ragtag freedom fighter for a noble, but doomed, cause than as "the weird old dude who talks to himself when he cuts our lawn" (as one teenager recently called him).

And then another thought occurred to him. Maybe he could salvage some sort of a *moral* victory by showing up at Tranquility Mortuary Services and proving to the mortician that he hadn't been blowing smoke when he claimed to be able to fix cremation ovens. If, for example, he went to the library, spent fifteen minutes studying how cremation ovens work, and absorbed just enough to seem competent, then he might be able to put over a good, satisfying fraud of his own! Hell, maybe he could get a credit card and take out an ad in *The Town Gazette*, letting everyone know that he was skilled in the repair of cremation ovens.

The Town wasn't very big, of course. So the ad would reach most of the populace. Bear in mind, it's not that Harry wanted to sell cremation oven repair services to the general public. He just wanted the townsfolk to know that such repair services were available at a moment's notice. (If they knew this, they'd feel emboldened to ask the mortician to repair the cremation oven, when he claimed it was broken. They wouldn't automatically go along with the upselling.)

And if they wouldn't automatically go along with the upselling, then they'd be frustrating the goals of a half-freak. And frustrating the goals of a half-freak was inherently valuable, as they were all (from Harry's point of view) irredeemably evil.

Some of you are probably thinking that this is a bizarre line of reasoning. You may be thinking that there should be a far simpler answer to the question: "Why didn't Harry just hang himself?"

For such readers, I offer this explanation: there are people for whom suicide is—realistically speaking—a possible fate, and there are people for whom suicide is only a subject for rumination (never to actually be attempted). I believe I am in the second category, and that Harry is there with me.

What evidence do I have for this belief? Well, as I've already explained at the beginning of this book, I have met Harry Meyers face-to-face. I believe we ruminators know when we've met another of our kind.

The Smell of the End of the World

Harry got out of the tub and started to pace around the house. He was still wet from the bathtub, still naked, still prune-fingered, and a little out of it. Were the curtains open? Could people see him waddling around in there?

Possibly, but he didn't care.

Up in the second-floor hallway, he stuck his head through the open door of Mother's room. He noticed, out of the corner of his eye, a neatly folded stack of men's trousers and underwear resting on her bureau. (The last pile of clothes she'd folded, before that final trip to the hospital.)

It took him quite a while to summon the courage to walk in and grab them, though. The room smelled sour. It wasn't the smell of slow death. Harry thought of it, instead, as The Smell of the End of the World.

By this, he didn't mean it was the smell of fire and cataclysm, but rather a smell halfway between that of sweat and that of ozone. It was the smell of ghosts. (At the risk of putting words into Harry's mouth, the smell of an insistent absence.) He could taste the odor, and it was palpable. It had tendrils that grew down into his stomach.

His hands and legs trembled as he picked up the stack of clothes. For some reason he couldn't quite articulate, he was scared to catch a glimpse of himself in the bureau's mirror. So he did an about face and made for the door.

As he was exiting the room, he dropped the clothes. When he

leaned down to pick them up, he became dizzy and hit his head against the door jamb. He let out a self-pitying growl and, in frustration, threw half of them down the hallway.

That was the final delay, though. By eleven forty-five, he was ready to take care of business. Not even a falling sky would keep him from his rightful destiny as a cremation oven repairman.

Starsputter-grind, 1,000 noobab skeirhs
Starsputter-grind, 1,000 noobab skeirhs
Starsputter-grind, 1,000 noobab skeirhs

The Town Library

I feel compelled to start off this chapter with an observation: libraries are not the same as they were when I was a child. Back then, there was an expectation that everyone entering those sacred halls would remain courteously silent for the length of their visit. If conversation was absolutely essential, then it was to be conducted in whispers. If, for whatever reason, a conversation was conducted at a volume louder than a whisper, the librarian would place her finger up to her lips and loudly go "Shhh!"

This etiquette was quite necessary, as the library was a place where people assembled to focus quietly on the written word. You came to the library for only three reasons: to read, to *find something to* read, or to research. If you came to do the latter, you needed a pencil, paper, the card catalog, and a few dollars in quarters to use the photocopy machine.

Nowadays, of course, almost-nobody comes to libraries for such noble reasons. They come to get out of the cold (because they're homeless). Or, they come to use the internet (because the online world is where most people live these days; thus, being off social networking is a kind of homelessness in its own right).

In my childhood, a library was essentially a Book Zoo. Hell, it was even better than the zoo, because the zoo didn't allow you to borrow the animals for two weeks at a time. In 2019, however, libraries have devolved into Book *Mausoleums.*

This might not be such a bad thing. After all, there's a certain dignity to a mausoleum, right?

Well, yes, ideally. But here's the thing: Book Mausoleums aren't like the well-kept mausoleums of chic internet moguls. They're more akin to the mausoleums of once-famous (but now-forgotten) nineteenth century actors; the kind of actors who received the applause of presidents in their lifetime, but now haven't even so much as a Wikipedia page to attest to the fact of their existence. Book Mausoleums are like mausoleums in once-prestigious neighborhoods that have fallen into decrepitude. They're like mausoleums that have been tagged with graffiti, broken into, and robbed.

I mention this because I want you to understand the type of environment Harry was likely to encounter at The Town Library in 2019, even under the best of circumstances. Now, imagine that same sort of setting (already degenerated from its past glory) suffering *further* degeneration during this Age of Half-Freaks, this Era of the Falling Sky.

Yes, it was far from pretty.

You see, even though Harry had been the only one with sufficiently acute hearing to detect the various half-cracks in reality (*softtinkle, rumblethunder*), EVERYONE saw/heard/felt the sky falling and so EVERYONE sought shelter whenever a new piece tore loose (*starsputter-grind, 1,000 noobab skeirhs*). The Town Library was known for its sturdy, mausoleum-like construction. In fact, a yellow-and-black Fallout Shelter sign remained affixed to the building (a relic of Cold War civil defense plans).

And so, a great number of Town residents poured in to seek shelter. Of course, the homeless were there en masse. But not *just* the homeless. Everyone in town, regardless of status, needed protection.

When Harry arrived, there was a line ten deep just to get in. Among those seeking shelter were the preacher from The Town Church, the exterminator from The Town Bug Assassins, and the owner of The Town Gun Shop.

The gun shop owner was uncharacteristically jumpy while queued up for entry. He was usually a gregarious, wholesome fellow. That morning, however, his pistol was in his right hand and he kept looking up, down, and all around for something to shoot.

Meanwhile, in his left hand, he held a heavy black sack. When he wasn't glancing around for something to shoot, he was scanning the crowd for a potential customer. He claimed the sack held "eight loaded handguns, cash to make change, and my cell phone and Square reader for folks who wanna use plastic." He kept badgering Harry to buy a pistol. "Ya look like ya need peace of mind, my friend. We're all gonna need some peace of mind, headin into this shelter, y'know? Well, let me tell ya five hundred dollars buys a LOT of peace of mind. Yeah, son! A LOT!"

Harry had no patience for such pushiness. He'd experienced more than his fair share of aggressive sales pitches lately. He wanted to punch the gun shop owner in the jaw, just to shut him up. But he felt it unwise to pick a fight with someone who was armed and edgy. So instead, he resorted to a verbal response.

"Now just listen up for a minute! I'm a workin man, see? I don't have the money or the time for that kinda shit right now. What do ya think I am? Some sorta Mr. T or somethin, firin off a machine gun at drug dealers? Ya think I'm some sorta Howlin Mad Murdock or George Peppard grenade-tossin fella? Nah. Nah. I'm not a member of the fuckin A team or B team or L-M-N-O-P team! I'm a workin man. I ain't made of money, and I didn't come here to buy a gun. I came here to look at an en-silo-pedia (sic)."

As the word "en-silo-pedia" left his mouth, he felt a new emotional

91

wind sweep over him. He was no longer exasperated, because that single word made him recall his ambition to learn a few things about cremation oven repair. He decided to do a little bragging.

"Ya see, I haven't taken out the advertisements yet, but I'm learnin to fix cremation ovens. And, let me tell ya somethin brother, cremation oven repairmen make BANK. Uh huh, BANK." His voice became confident, even proud, as he took on the happy burden of promoting his non-existent expertise.

The gun shop owner frowned. Harry interpreted that as an expression of jealousy.

He was probably right. I think the gun shop owner took pride in having chosen a line of work ideally suited for apocalyptic conditions. I think he felt superior to the rest of the town, because it had taken real foresight to defy the vocational aptitude tests that had said he should be a mailman, instead.

So when Harry showed up with boasts of his own, about a line of work that seemed similarly well-suited to catastrophe, the gun shop owner resented it. He turned his back to Harry and started making his sales pitch to other folks in line. (Somehow, during their conversation, the two of them had fallen farther back. Now, instead of ten people in front of Harry, there were twenty-five.)

As if all of this wasn't bad enough, Harry's nostrils were soon assaulted by the (over-familiar, apparently inescapable) odor of shit. This time, however, there was no bleach scent to counter it. It was earthy, animalistic shit. It was shit mixed with mud, and caked onto the naked legs of an emaciated old woman in a halter top, miniskirt, and orthopedic shoes. She extended an arthritic claw and slapped Harry on the shoulder. "I'm sellin newspapers for twenny-five cents, the same price they were back in nineteen eighty-seven. Ya want one? Just twenny-five cents. Just twenny-five cents."

The falling sky noise again:

Starsputter-grind, 1,000 noobab skeirhs

Starsputter-grind, 1,000 noobab skeirhs

Starsputter-grind, 1,000 noobab skeirhs

Another piece had come loose, this one directly overhead. The queue panicked, screamed, and pushed each other out of the way as they ran inside. Some abandoned the door altogether and smashed their way through windows instead. As they climbed in, they were treated like an invading army. "Ain't no more room in here," an old man said. Then he laughed and burned the shelter-seekers with a lit cigar.

The gun shop owner tried to restore order by emptying his pistol into the air. Alas, that had the opposite of the intended effect. When members of The Nefarious Town Gang saw he had to reload, they mugged him. (Guns, ammo, cash, Square reader, cell phone, all gone.) Harry didn't feel the least bit sorry for him.

The shit smell. The gnarled hand, insistent, asking if Harry wanted to buy a paper.

Starsputter-grind, 1,000 noobab skeirhs

More screams. More laughs. More sounds of shattering glass.

"Just twenny five cents, the same price they were back in nineteen eighty-seven. Ya want one?"

Starsputter-grind, 1,000 noobab skeirhs

Starsputter-grind, 1,000 noobab skeirhs

"Ya want one? Ya want one? Ya want one?"

Harry was about to wind back and slap the shit out of the geriatric newsie, when he was shocked into stillness. Her nose was wrinkled up in a very peculiar way; a way he'd seen a nose wrinkled up many times before. Also, her neck seemed to swell out like that of a ribbing frog.

The old woman dragged one leg behind her, shambling closer. There was a gleam in her eye he hadn't noticed before. "Maybe ya wanna take a look at it before ya buy it, eh? Maybe ya don't trust that it has good shit in it to read. Maybe you're a skeptic eh?"

She pushed a copy of *The Town Gazette* into his hands and started to sing to herself. "A skeptic, antiseptic, skep-tick repellent, skeleton pick, skelet-off pick. A skeptical septical skeptic!" The tune to this nonsensical ditty seemed half-familiar, like a backwards version of "Amazing Grace".

The *Gazette* was unorthodox in that it published all obituaries on the front page. However, if you think about it, this makes a lot of sense. Why should a local newspaper devote such prominent space to boring stories about the election of new officers for The Town Birdwatching Society or discussion of pending amendments to The Zoning Commission's bylaws? How many residents are chomping at the bit to read that sort of dreck?

People buy small town newspapers to find out who died, so why not devote the front page to large photos of the deceased and the first sentence of their obit? Why not give them a little teaser of what they really want to know, to encourage them to buy the paper and get the full story back on page A17! Undoubtedly, this savvy strategy is what kept the *Gazette*'s circulation healthy when so many other local papers were going the way of the dodo. Undoubtedly, this is why the *Gazette* could afford to keep the price at "only twenny-five cents".

The reason I mentioned all of that was to set the stage for the next disturbing revelation. You see, the headline on the front page read:

ONE BY CANCER, ONE BY CAR

Below the headline (extending all the way down to the fold), were two black-and-white photographs. The one on the left was Mother's mug shot from her most recent DWI arrest.

Of course, her *nose* was scrunched up in a very peculiar manner and her *throat* was swollen like the throat of a ribbiting frog. That much was par for the course, in her mug shots. But the photo in that morning's *Gazette* was even worse than usual, because it also made Mother's *eyes* look like they were on the verge of popping out of her head and her *mouth* look like it was about to spew cackles. (Apparently that was the only picture of her the newspaper had on file, and they had no qualms about using it out of context.)

The photo on the right showed a much younger woman who looked familiar. According to the caption, it had been cropped from a picture taken only two days earlier, when she had won a fifth-place ribbon at The Town Fair for her cross-stitch of an oxygen machine. Her hair was dark and shiny, and she looked like she took good care of herself. Harry guessed she was only a b cup, but he could deal with that.

Was that who he thought it was? Could it be? *Her*? Dead? "By Car?"

There was only one small detail that made him pause before concluding that it was the nurse from Three East: the woman's face was distorted. Was it just his imagination? Some wonky printing error? Or, was it actually the case that one of her eyes was positioned significantly lower than the other? Could a person's eyeball really grow out of their cheekbone? He seemed to be observing evidence of such a condition at that very moment. But how could it have happened?

An uncomfortable answer popped into Harry's head: the nurse had been transformed into a.... Harry wouldn't even let himself think the word. Not in reference to that nurse, with her soft, pale skin. *She might've been transformed into somethin that rhymes with 'laugh-weak'*, he told himself, and left it at that.

That whole line of thinking gave him a shudder, so he forced himself to think about other frustrating questions. Why was Mother's obituary already in the paper? Wasn't it going to be his job to write that up? Was this just another money-grubbing scheme of the mortician's? Was he going to try and sneak a fee into the bill for writing the obit? Was an obit even needed since Mother was going to be cremated? Had that half-freak son of a bitch announced that she was going to be getting a "full Christian burial", despite Harry's insistence that he could fix the cremation oven?

"Hey Mr. Skeptic-Trekpic-Shrek Tick, that's twenny-five cents. I'll scream for the po-po if ya don't hand over your twenny-five cents! Give it to me now! Gimme! Gimme my money! Twenny-five cents! Gimme! Gimme!"

Harry got out his wallet, and that made the old woman shut up. He took out a wrinkled, greasy dollar bill and gave it to her.

She grinned. "Now you'll be able to read all about my sister. She's the one in the mug shot. They buried her this mornin and that's why I'm so late with deliverin the papers. But it was worth it. So worth it! A backhoe dug the grave, and a crane lowered this expensive-lookin casket into there. She always was a money-grubber, that one! Anyway, the crane lowered her into the ground, and then the backhoe covered her all up, and then they were done. I stayed all the way until the end so I could dance on her grave. And oh, how I danced!"

Harry's aunt commenced to give him a monstrous demonstration. Her arthritic joints clacked together, like castanets, as her arms and legs swayed. These appendages moved in a manner that was obviously, well... *off*. Their bones and tendons and ligaments had been shattered, pulled, and torn. One foot hung at a right angle to its leg. During a ghastly pirouette, Harry spotted a compound rib fracture.

Each of her movements further destabilized the fragile sky.

Starsputter-grind, 1,000 noobab skeirhs.

Starsputter-grind, 1,000 noobab skeirhs.

She was clearly more than a half-freak. She was a three-quarters freak, and she was Harry's blood relation!

"Oh, how I glanced for a chance to dance on her grave! Chanced for a dance to…."

Did she know he was her nephew? She'd never met him, so why should she? But, on the other hand, she seemed to be greatly enjoying his dismay. Would she be getting that much gratification from mind fucking a random customer?

Perhaps. One never knew with three-quarters freaks.

"Lance-a-dance-boil! Lance-a-dance-goil! Lance-a-dance-in-a-pot-five-days-old!"

"Hey! HEY! Get away from me!" Harry yelled. "Leave me alone! Leave me ALONE!"

"Blanche-a-loyal-dance-a-Rose-dance-a-Dorothy-ranch-a-lanced-Sophia-Loren-Dance-a-a-a-dance-a-Golden-Coffin-Girl-in-her-hole-dance-ON-the-hole-and-take-a-SHIT, or else lose IT! Dance-a-dance-a…"

Harry had heard enough. He didn't even wait to get change back for his dollar. If what his aunt said were true, he had been defeated by the mortician. Reality was falling apart and there was nothing he could do about it. There was only one course of action left for him. He would go home and masturbate to the nurse's obituary picture. He would use scissors, beforehand, to cut out the offending eye and paste it back into its proper position.

Was it Really the Nurse, or Did Some Other Woman Die?

Honestly, I don't know for certain.

What I do know for certain is this: Harry saw a woman on the front page of *The Town Gazette* who *looked like the nurse* (the same hairstyle, the same dark shade of hair, the same boob size). She was even into sewing and crafts, as evidenced by the caption's mention of her mediocre showing in a needlepoint competition. Moreover, the needlepoint itself (depicting an oxygen machine) seems to have been inspired by work in a hospital setting such as Three East.

And, lest we forget, Harry's Prophetic Dream foretold of a situation in which Harry's mother and another woman would be caught up together in the same funereal peril. ("She's with me and she's scared! She's with me and she's scared!") Surely, the dream had prophesied a situation in which both of them had wanted cremation but were forced to undergo the rigors (no pun intended) of embalming and "full Christian burial".

But let's say that, by some twist of fate, it actually wasn't the nurse in that picture. That it was, instead, someone with a similar appearance, a similar workplace, and a similar hobby. Would it really make that much of a difference?

Knowing Harry the way I do, I don't think it would. His erotic imagination had been fired simply by the resemblance alone. So what if she wasn't *exactly* the nurse? She was close enough to give him a boner on the way home. After the previous night's episode of erectile dysfunction, he wasn't about to look a gift horse in the mouth.

Okay, So She Was Probably the Nurse from Three East. But…

…had she actually been transformed into a half-freak? Or, had her photo merely been distorted during the printing process?

For that matter, did the half-freaks actually exist? Or, did they only exist in Harry's mind? Had he been hallucinating this whole time?

These are all very interesting questions that have probably been on your mind, off and on, for a while now. They've been on my mind, too. However, I can tell you, with one hundred percent certainty, that he was not hallucinating. Not even in the slightest.

You may be wondering how I can be so sure of this. We established in the very first chapter that Harry's brain was clammy, wobbly, sick, and above all *moldy*. And wouldn't a moldy brain be vulnerable to hallucinations?

Well, yes. But we have to consider this inconvenient aspect of the story: if Harry had been hallucinating, then he would have been the only one in town who saw the sky fall. But the chaotic scene outside the library clearly demonstrates that the entire town was in a panic. Are we prepared to say that each and every resident of The Town had been hallucinating, as well? That thousands of them had fallen victim to synchronized insanity?

As Harry himself might say: Nah. Nah.

Yes, his brain was moldy, but I think this moldiness had more to do with his sexual compulsions, poor personal hygiene, clinical depression, lack of social skills, and, yes, perhaps even some "special knees". Nonetheless, his sensations and perceptions were every bit as real as your own. He was completely in touch with reality (whatever that means).

Now that this truth has been communicated, let's dive back into fiction.

This Land of Loathsome Vertigo

Harry's head felt like a helium balloon. By this, I mean that it wasn't so much *attached* to his neck as it was *floating* above it. I believe this feeling was a result of overstimulation. He had seen too many sights while in line outside the library. He had felt too many emotions there, as well. His throat (and lungs) were sore from screaming. Even his erection ached.

He wanted to immediately correct the nurse's obituary picture, so that her eye was in the correct position. (Then he could proceed to jack off to a pretty girl instead of a half-freak.) However, every time he opened a kitchen drawer to find a pair of scissors, he found nothing but broken plastic utensils and mouse turds. Every time he closed a drawer, a stack of mail on the counter quivered and fell.

He had to use an old steak knife instead. Holding it like a scalpel, he slowly traced the curve of her misplaced eyeball. The result was, as you might imagine, less than ideal. His hand shook the entire time. As a result, his incision was far more ragged and crinkled than he would have liked.

Nonetheless, he proceeded to the pasting stage of the operation. This part went a bit easier, as he always knew where he kept his tube of Elmer's Glue. It was upstairs in his nightstand, along with his porno mags and construction paper. He grabbed the tube and went to work.

His dick became ramrod stiff.

In his zeal, however, he used too much glue. It oozed out from behind the nurse's eye. When it dried, it left a scaly residue that made the nurse look like she'd suffered from eczema. Even worse, he'd accidentally pasted the eye at a slight angle. (A thirteen-degree angle, actually.)

Even if he were able to somehow look past those mistakes, there was another problem that simply couldn't be ignored: he had created an eye-shaped hole on the nurse's cheekbone. In his fervor, he hadn't thought everything through. His dick drooped.

He howled. Kicked things. Stubbed his toe. Howled some more. The bedroom's stale air tightened around him like a straitjacket.

He rolled up *The Town Gazette* and threw it at his window. It got snared in the dusty mini blinds. He grabbed a thick porno mag out of his nightstand and threw it at *The Town Gazette*. It knocked the newspaper flat onto the ground. Mother looked up at him. Nose scrunched. Throat swollen. Eyes on the verge of popping out of her head. Mouth on the verge of spewing cackles.

He read the two obituaries. Though Mother's life had been quite different from the nurse's, the newspaper used the exact same hackneyed phrases to describe them both. Both were "fondly remembered by neighbors for their smiling faces". Both were "now enjoying their heavenly reward". The remains of both had been disposed of via "full Christian burial provided by Tranquility Mortuary Services, The Nation's leading post-mortem care provider". It was as though the half-freak mortician had used the same boilerplate for all obituaries, and had merely inserted a different name in each.

Harry turned his gaze back to the front-page photographs. He wanted to look at Mother's picture and cry, the way a good son should. However, much to his alarm, he found that cum trickled out of his eyes, instead of tears. Even his grief was, against his will, quite indecent.

Understandably, this made him lose his erection. Understandably, this made him bite his arm and pull his hair. Understandably, this made him wobble downstairs to grab a box of matches. Understandably, this made him wander around the house and set every room on fire.

Mother = fire. Fire = purification. She may have been buried, yes. But perhaps he could undo the harm of burial by cremating her obituary picture, and cremating her house, and hoping that the fires might spread so that The Town, The Region, and even The Whole World might catch fire, too.

When Mother died, reality had died. Yes, that explained it all. Reality had croaked, and then—as the days proceeded—it decayed. Just as a corpse becomes ever-more disfigured with the advance of rot, so too had rotting reality become disfigured.

A three-quarters freak? A falling sky? Both were clear signs of decomposition! And not even "full Christian burial" could stop that process! Only cremation could. That, I think, is what Harry hoped to achieve. It's not that he wanted to burn *himself* alive. It's that he hated the rotting reality in which he was trapped, and wanted to put *it* out of *its* misery. He wanted to cremate reality's corpse, and then perform the sacrifices that would make certain its ghost never returned to haunt him.

The End

(Well, sort of. Turn the page for another section, the truly final section, titled **After the End**.)

After the End

So, to repeat, Harry's arson wasn't a suicide attempt. It was an attempt to escape the rot in which he'd been trapped. And it succeeded! Now that the story is over, he's no longer stuck inside the cacophonous, fetid world I fabricated for your amusement.

(I should add that I don't mean "amusement" in a shallow sense of mere entertainment, but also in the richer sense, of providing a meaningful aesthetic experience. Yes. That, too. Yes, yes.

Harry visits me less and less these days. The last *confirmed* sighting was over two weeks ago, shortly after I'd finished writing **This Land of Loathsome Vertigo**.

He wouldn't even speak to me that day. He just stood in the corner of my office and scowled. I suppose he thought that would torment me; that I'd be upset at the silent treatment. That I would rack my brain to figure out what I'd done to offend him.

But is it really that hard to figure out? I knew he'd hated that world of half-freaks, death, and falling skies. I knew that, even though he'd extricated himself from that world, he would go on to carry lasting emotional scars from his time there. I knew he resented that I'd cast him as a creepy sad sack, a compulsive masturbator, a dupe, etc. I knew he resented that I'd made his life out to be a dark comedy. The angry, hurt expression on his face was meant as a condemnation.

Now, in my defense, Harry has only himself to blame. *He's* the one who set the stage for this characterization, with all his banter about Erin Burnett's "coochie-coo" and bragging about being "the Badass Knight of Blood and Cum". *He's* the one who came, by his own free will, to my office. I didn't go out searching for him.

That's all beside the point, though. The fact is, I believe him to be more than just a creepy sad sack. More than just a compulsive masturbator. More than just a dupe. Did he not see that reflected on the page? Yes, he is a half-comical, half-tragic character. Yes, his foes are (by and large) half-comical, half-menacing characters. But the comedy isn't meant to completely strip him of dignity.

One little caveat: I *do* believe the nurse had every right to feel revolted by his touch. If I had been in her shoes, I'd have felt the same way. Nevertheless, Harry's desires (to touch another person, to grieve without being exploited, to have a little cushion of financial security, to reject a reality that is breaking apart were quite natural. They were human desires, frustrated by a pseudo-human world.

I wrote that last paragraph a few days ago. As is my custom, I printed out the manuscript so I could re-read it for editing. I left it on my desk overnight, in its own stack (apart from all the others on my sloppy desk) and left the front door unlocked in the hope that Harry might try to sneak in and read it. I knew I was on his shitlist, but I figured that—if he read that last paragraph—he might come to appreciate the depth which I'd actually granted him.

This morning, I realized what a foolish expectation that had been. When I came into my office to begin editing, I did, indeed, smell his presence: the body odor, tooth decay, and pomade. He'd been there. Yeah. Yeah. He'd been there, yes indeedy-do! But he left behind two outward and visible signs of his inward and spiritual disgust.

First, he'd taken a brown sharpie to the manuscript and vandalized the title of this book's first chapter. It now read: **The ~~Broken Brain~~ Satanic Heart of ~~Harry Meyers~~ Nicole Cushing**.

Secondly, he'd duct taped a matchbook to the wall over my desk, and also duct taped a note next to the matchbook. It read: "You do it or I will."

I suppose I was meant to feel frightened, and I did. A feverish, half-real heaviness lingered all around me, as if my blood had turned to magma; as if my heart suddenly weighed a hundred pounds. But I was also confused. What did he think I was, some sort of Wicked Witch of the Midwest? Some sort of devil-worshipping fire bug? What exactly did he want me to burn? The manuscript? The house? Both? Or was he demanding I commit self-immolation?

Of course, I did none of those things. Nor will I do any of those things in the future.

But I know that, someday, Harry will strike back against me with fire. Maybe he'll enlist Ellie from *The Sadist's Bible* and the young man from *Mr. Suicide* as his accomplices. Maybe all three of them will re-enact the pivotal scene from that old movie *The Burning Bed*. Maybe he'll wait until I've created many more twisted, tortured characters, so that he can raise an entire platoon against me!

Would any of my characters refuse to join such a mob? Would any come to my defense? No. That would be like Dr. Moreau hoping for loyalty from his beasts!

My only hope is that, when the time comes, I prove to be as "Satanic" as Harry thinks I am. I'm thinking especially in terms of the Satan in Dante's *Inferno*. Maybe I'll blow a mighty, freezing wind that'll extinguish the fire. Maybe I'll sprout black wings. Maybe I'll grow two additional heads, and spend eternity devouring traitors, as I remember—all the while—that I am a traitor to normality, myself.

ABOUT THE AUTHOR

Nicole Cushing is the Bram Stoker Award® winning author of *Mr. Suicide* and a two-time nominee for the Shirley Jackson Award. Various reviewers have described her work as "brutal," "cerebral," "transgressive," "taboo," "groundbreaking," and "mind-bending".

This Is Horror has said that she is "quickly becoming a household name for horror fans." She has also garnered praise from Jack Ketchum, *Rue Morgue Magazine*, Thomas Ligotti, and Poppy Z. Brite.

GRIMSCRIBE PRESS

Milton Keynes UK
Ingram Content Group UK Ltd.
UKHW021344300923
429699UK00024B/717